BEYOND

THE

SHADOWS

2023

Barbara,

all the best
and enjoy
reading !

Take care,

DeAnn

BEYOND

THE

SHADOWS

DEANN DALEY HOLCOMB

atmosphere press

CHAPTER ONE

He'd seen her in the club before, all soft curves and long legs, but the timing hadn't been right. The sweet adrenalin rush of what was to come had just started to flow and he'd been ready to make his move when her date showed up. He backed off, disappointed but willing to wait for his next prize. There would be another night.

Jenny Latham closed her eyes and rocked to the beat of the music. Showing off her sexy, short, black dress, she enjoyed the music from the Jason Aldean-type country band while she stood at the bar waiting for another drink.

Jenny looked outside at the swarm of people on the patio. It was a pleasant night, even though the summer heat was starting to creep in. Inside the popular nightclub, Mickey's, it was getting crowded and the bar was full of people socializing, partying, searching for someone to party with. It smelled of fresh polished leather, perfume and lingering smoke. Instantly, she felt him standing close behind her. He pressed forward slightly to give his drink order to the bartender. Her excitement washed over her and her tummy warmed, but it had nothing to do with alcohol.

Jenny turned, looked up at him and smiled her dazzling white smile.

He nodded, backed away to pay for his beer.

"Hi Jeremy," Jenny said, smiling.

"Hey, Jenny, good to see you too."

She'd seen him here before. They had talked a couple of times, nothing serious. He was over 6'2", lean and muscular with black hair and piercing blue eyes. She noticed how big his hands were when he reached over to take his beer from the bartender. She didn't know why, but it turned her on.

"Are you alone?" Jeremy asked.

"No, my date's in the restaurant. I just wanted to check out what was happening in here and get another drink," Jenny said.

"Your date won't buy you a drink?"

Jenny laughed.

She'd never understand why she did it, but she noticed the pen on the bar. She reached over and wrote down her cell phone number on the napkin, and laid it back on the bar in front of him.

He picked up the napkin and put it in the back pocket of his jeans.

"Give me a call when you get a chance and we can meet for lunch or something."

"That sounds right on my agenda. Call you later," Jeremy replied.

Jenny waved goodbye, turned and walked away, back to the table to join her date for the night. Jenny paused in the aisle as a couple was being seated. She thought her date, Johnny Watson, was good looking, and she knew he had money, but he didn't do anything to turn her on physically. No, her Mr. tall, dark and handsome was who Jenny wanted to be with. She wondered if the thrill of what she'd done added to her excitement. Jenny had never acted on a whim when it came to men. She'd always been careful. Her girlfriends would laugh at her, telling her to loosen up and have fun.

Jeremy might not even call, but it was a chance she was

willing to take.

Johnny went to the restroom before dinner arrived. He wasn't happy when he glanced into the bar and saw his friend, Jeremy, talking to Jenny. Johnny and Jeremy were always in competition when it came to a pretty woman. He sat down at the table moments before she arrived, sipping his scotch, and waiting.

Jenny smiled at Johnny when she sat down. They talked about their work day before their steaks arrived. She ordered her third glass of wine, more than she usually drank, but then she figured it would be easier to put up with him. Watson decided not to say anything about seeing her talking to his friend. Time went by slowly. All she could think about was her friend in the bar.

Once dinner was over and they were getting ready to leave the restaurant, walking towards the front door of the restaurant club, Jenny couldn't bring herself to look into the club as they passed by, but she could hear the music blaring loud, a Keith Urban song, "Without You." The disc jockey had continued the country music theme and had the country night going strong. She figured by now the party was underway, since bodies were lined up against the wall on the way out.

During the drive back to Jenny's house there wasn't much conversation. She wanted to get home fast.

All Watson could think about was getting her in bed. Usually the pay for taking a woman out for a fancy dinner was a quick one and then Johnny would be on his way. The spark, thrill for him, was the thrill of conquering. He wasn't sure about Jenny though. He couldn't get a read on her.

Johnny got out of his black Lexus and walked around to open the door. He helped Jenny out of the car, then grabbed the back of her head and crushed his lips down on her mouth. It was a kiss to let her know what he wanted. She tasted like the sweet liqueur she had for an after dinner drink, and it turned him on instantly. He had to hand it to her; she kissed back just as hard. He pulled back to look at her, knowing the invitation was coming.

"Johnny, dinner was wonderful, but I need to get going," Jenny told him. "I have a fashion show coming up, and I need to get up early."

He tried to hide his disappointment, although he was seething inside. How could he have been so stupid, he wondered. "Sure, I'll see you around."

"Thank you again for dinner. I'll see myself in," Jenny said as she walked toward the front door of her condo.

Johnny got in his SUV, so angry he didn't even watch to see if Jenny made it inside safely. He hit his hands on his steering wheel. He remembered that woman named Lori he met at Starbucks the other day. She had been there with Jenny. He didn't think it was a chance meeting. He felt like the women had been waiting for him. But Jenny was the sexy one. He may have wasted most of the evening on the wrong chick. He knew the other one would let him in without a second thought. Watson just had to remember where she lived. Close by, right? Going through his glove box, Watson searched for the paper that had her name and address on it. He felt certain he'd written it down.

Jenny unlocked her door and let herself in, closed the door, turned on the alarm, then turned on the front porch lights, dimming the lights in the entrance hall. She walked toward the living room and had just lit two candles when the doorbell rang.

Jenny jumped in surprise. Had Johnny come back? Her alarms inside her were going off as she walked toward the front door. She had grabbed her cell phone in case she needed to call 911.

Jenny peeked out the peephole in her front door.

She took a step back in surprise. "What the heck? What's

Jeremy doing here?"

Her nerves didn't calm. She was puzzled. How did he find me? she wondered.

Jenny slowly unlocked and opened the front door.

"Hey girl," Jeremy said, a big smile on his face.

"How did you find me?" Jenny asked.

"Oh, I have my ways," Jeremy said as he started laughing.

Finally, Jenny reacted. "Oh well, come on in Jeremy." She held the door open wider. Jeremy walked in, and she closed the door and locked it.

Six months later, chaos breaks out.

It was five in the morning when the phone rang. Lance Harris, Chief Homicide Detective and Chief of the Dallas Homicide Division coughed and groaned, nearly knocking the lamp off the nightstand, as he reached to pick up his cell phone. He'd been asleep for less than three hours and feeling the effects of the previous night. "Oh, hell," he muttered as he grabbed his cell phone, his hangover roaring in his head.

"Hello? Yeah, okay, I'll be right there," Harris told the dispatcher.

His day was not off to a good start. As he climbed out of bed and reached for his blue jeans on the chair, his cell phone rang again. Caller ID identified Matthew Shaw, a Dallas patrol officer.

"Shaw, what's up?"

"Just got to that new scene, Chief," Shaw said. "We've got another one."

Harris groaned, "Don't tell me this one's got a Smiley Face sticker too."

"Afraid so."

"Damn. Make sure and keep the media back from the scene. I'm on my way," Lance said, punching the end-call button as fast as the last word was uttered.

Another female body with a smiley face sticker stuck on her neck.

On his way to the crime scene, Lance wondered if the pounding in his head would ever go away. He knew it was stupid as hell to go out on the town like he did last night, playing pool, poker and drinking scotch, but he needed a break from this latest murder investigation only to have another victim turn up hours later.

The 911 call came in a few minutes before 5am after an early morning jogger found the body of a young woman in the park. On her neck, the killer left a smiley face sticker, like the murder last week. It had a black background and bright yellow face on it.

Two murders in two weeks. Shaking his head, Lance knew the media will be in a frenzy.

Lance was the first detective to arrive. The patrolmen, under Shaw's direction, set up a perimeter around the crime scene.

"Has the medical examiner been notified?" Lance asked Shaw as he walked up.

"He'll be here in fifteen minutes."

"Send Detective Sanchez to me as soon as he arrives."

Lance walked down the sidewalk to the wooded area where the woman's body was.

Rock Port Lake and Park was a popular place for runners and bikers. Despite the bushes and large mesquite trees that shadowed the sidewalk where joggers ran daily, Lance noted that the killer did not try very hard to hide the body. Was the killer in a hurry? He knew that could be important! A statement made by the killer.

Lance stepped in close to her and looked down at the victim, feeling the wave of anger wash over him every time he came across a murdered woman. He could tell she was young and had been beautiful. Which made it even worse.

There didn't seem to be any signs of a struggle. Had she freely gone with him?

Had the killer murdered her somewhere else and then dumped the body here?

Lance closed his eyes for a few moments, trying to concentrate on the few clues that he had and to try and get a feel for what happened. Lance knelt down closer to examine the body.

He considered the horror of what this young woman went through before she died.

Medical Examiner Spencer Wyatt would have to confirm what he suspected. The victim was naked, except for the torn blouse, an important piece of evidence that was to be kept from the media. And there was that damn smiley face sticker!

Lance thought, the murderer raped the young woman before she was killed. The way her body laid on the ground. If his suspicions were right, they were in trouble. It meant there could be a serial killer out there. He walked around the body, trying to find any evidence the killer left behind, looking for footprints in the dirt, cigarettes, torn paper, clothing, anything.

He heard Reid's voice behind him, talking.

Harris looked up, waving him over. Detective Reid Sanchez, second in command under Lance, stopped when he reached Lance's side. He looked down at the young woman. Reid's expression was one of hatred for whoever had done this.

Lance knew if anyone could help him find the murderer it would be Reid. He was egotistical, hard-hitting and cavalier with a no-nonsense attitude. Reid was what the women would describe as 'virile, strong and brave.' Lance thought Reid was one of the best homicide detectives he had ever worked with. They'd become close friends over the years and had become known as "the team," within the police department.

"This is tough," Reid said.

"Find out if we have any missing person reports on any women in the area," Lance said to Reid. "As soon as we identify her we need to reconstruct the last forty eight hours of her life."

"On it. Not looking good is it?"

"I think it's time to issue an official alert. I'll talk to the Chief when I get back."

"Chief's not going to like that. You know how concerned he is about scaring the public."

Reid knew Lance didn't care much for Dallas Police Chief Ben Lewis.

To Lance it felt like Lewis was more interested in the Dallas social scene than running a police department. Lance suspected Lewis knew how he felt about him. The two men had issues between them and it involved the chief's wife.

If it turned out to be a serial killer, Lewis would come down hard on him for not having made an arrest.

Reid turned and headed for his car as Lance called out to him, "Ask me if I give a shit." Turning his attention back to the park, Lance watched the crime scene investigators, who had arrived, do their job. They were meticulously going over the ground area surrounding the woman, searching for any evidence the killer left behind, taking photographs of anything suspicious that might be evidence.

Spencer arrived and Lance watched him examining the body, waiting for several minutes to hear his initial reaction.

"Hey, Harris, I need to show you something," Spencer, the ME said. "It looks like a small puncture wound on the inside of her thigh. It could be a break for us."

Lance didn't comment, waiting for Wyatt to continue. The ME was not only a good friend, but Lance respected him and his opinion as the Dallas County Medical Examiner.

"I think it's the same person. I suspect the victim was raped like the others because of the bruising. I'll know more when I get her body back to the morgue. We'll run toxicology tests to see what was in her body: alcohol, drugs, or if he drugged her. Depending on how long she has been here, it will determine if we can find out if she was given the 'date rape' drug."

"We need to identify her ASAP. I have Reid looking into any missing persons reports to see if anyone has contacted the police in the last twenty four hours."

"Well, she hasn't been dead long, I can tell you that. Maybe a couple of hours. I'll know more when I get her back."

"I'll be in my office. Call me when you have a preliminary report."

Details of the investigation swirled in Lance's mind as he headed to his truck parked behind the crime scene tape to get gloves to help look for evidence. The media started to show up. Word was out. He wondered how this tragedy could happen with the increased police manpower on the streets, stepped-up patrols of the parks, along with the relentless media attention. That wasn't what disturbed him the most. These brutal killings were too similar to a past murder investigation. A past he wanted to forget.

He needed to get all of the equipment out of his truck.

Lance would make sure to check on Johnny Watson, the man sitting on death row at the Huntsville prison, convicted six months ago of committing some of the worst crimes in Texas history. Lance was one of the detectives responsible for Watson being behind bars in the Texas state prison.

Watson killed seven women before the police stopped him.

Guilty memories and the faces of the murdered young women snaked into Lance's mind, sometimes without his control. Lance would always feel guilty for not being able to arrest Watson before his brutal attacks increased. Watson had become a suspect when a young lady came in to the police department, accusing Watson of raping her the night before.

She said she had gone to dinner with Watson and when they returned to her house, Watson wouldn't take no for an answer. Then, there had been the witnesses that placed Watson with Jenny Latham the night before she was found murdered.

Lance constantly saw the faces of the young women in his mind. At the trial the prosecution hung photographs of the murder victims on a peg board, so the jury could look at them every day. The grief suffered by the victims' families was devastating as they sat, looked and listened to the testimony day after day. Pushing the images away, Lance pondered the similarities in the murders then and what was happening now. The past and present, too close, too eerie. Too much alike.

Watson's signature had been a smiley face sticker, always left on her neck. The victim had been naked, except for what sometimes appeared to be a torn blouse. Evidence that never came out at the trial and Lance had been able to keep it under wraps all this time. Until now.

This time the media found out about the smiley face sticker and had gone wild, tagging the latest killer the Smiley Face Killer. Exactly what Lance was afraid would happen. The reporters still didn't know the victim had been found naked.

If Lance ever discovered the idiot detective that had let that information slip to the media, there would be hell to pay.

Could Watson be talking to someone on the outside?

The Watson murders were nearly identical to what was happening now. Lance wouldn't put it past the sick bastard. He figured he could make the three hour trek to the Huntsville prison tomorrow, depending on what his investigators were able to come up with today.

Back at the scene, protective gloves on, Lance and the

other detectives went to work searching and photographing anything that might be unusual, any evidence that could lead them to the murderer.

Three hours later, as Lance walked back to his truck, leaving Spencer and the crime tech investigators at the scene, several of the news reporters yelled his name, hoping for an interview.

The vultures had arrived.

He waved his arm, jumped in his truck and sped off. Let the police communications department handle the media.

Four hours after getting the call, Lance was on his way to his office at the downtown Dallas police headquarters. Lance would have to wait for what evidence they had gathered at the scene to come in.

Chemicals, metals, drugs, biological evidence gathered, shoe impressions, any DNA results, hopefully from the puncture wound Spencer had found inside her leg and hopefully fingerprints. A crime scene investigator had been diligently taking photographs of the scene and all of the evidence being gathered.

Twenty minutes later as Lance walked inside the police department building, a blast of frigid air from the office air conditioner hit him, in contrast with the humid spring weather outside. Lance waved at the police desk commander, Curt Rosen, as he continued down the hall towards his office.

Curt waved back.

Lance figured word had spread throughout the police station about the latest killing. He could hear the television on Rosen's back desk that he usually played. He told Lance it helped him get ready for the day, listening to the morning news.

Even though it was around nine in the morning, there was already a media fury with sketchy details being broadcast all over the Dallas-Fort Worth radio and television stations. All the negative attention and another unsolved murder meant a low-key atmosphere inside police headquarters.

Lance stopped in at the breakroom to grab a cup of coffee, hoping to clear his head from the lack of sleep and from the effects of last night. There was an untamed, charismatic, sexual presence about Lance.

Standing at six-foot two and muscular from working out at the gym, Lance was dangerously handsome with brown hair and green eyes. His smile could disarm you and when he was angry, his expression could stop you in your tracks. Close friends described Lance as cool, detached and unemotional. True, but there was always an exception.

Lance casually entered his office, walked to his desk and stopped in his tracks. He couldn't put his coffee cup down.

There she was, asleep on the couch in his office. This was dangerous.

Claire McKenzie looked breathtakingly beautiful with her brown hair flowing off the couch pillow. Her jacket barely covered her exquisite body, but it did not matter. Lance remembered. He looked at her face, thinking about her sweet smile, brown eyes and round lips. It had been six months since they were together.

As though she could feel his penetrating eyes on her, Claire abruptly sat up on the couch, trying to cover the front of her dress that had opened up, revealing the curves of her breasts.

Lance stood still, watching, as she tried to cover herself with her jacket, saying nothing.

Claire felt his anger as she looked into those beautiful green eyes that were shooting daggers at her. Maybe this wasn't such a good idea, Claire stood up from the couch.

Claire was petite, with a tiny hourglass figure and long brown hair flowing down her back compared to the tall, athletic warrior-looking Lance. Briefly, it flashed through her mind how they fit perfectly together, thinking about the last time he'd held her in his arms.

Earlier that morning, television news reporter Claire McKenzie begged her assignments editor to transfer her from reporting on the emergency airplane landing story at the Dallas-Fort Worth International Airport to report on this latest murder.

Claire, her news photographer, Chandler, and the live truck engineer, heard the police alert broadcast on the scanners while they were preparing to do a live shot for the Channel Two early morning newscast.

She'd felt faint when she heard Lance's voice calling for Reid to report to the murder scene.

Claire's chest ached with emotion. It was the longing, the sadness she always experienced whenever she heard his voice, saw him on television doing an interview or when she read about him in the paper. Claire remembered every touch, every moment they were together. Although she tried to deny her feelings, the attraction was still there.

"What the hell are you doing here?" Lance reacted loudly. "I thought they had you doing feature stories at the zoo."

Lance's harsh tone scared her. Claire then realized he had been watching her on television.

"I'm doing a follow up on the murder. I wanted to get with you on any new information for my story."

"You can go through the communications officer like everyone else. You know I can't show favoritism. By the way, how did you get in here and what are you doing asleep on my couch?"

Nervous and shaken by Lance's outburst, Claire's words spilled out faster than she wanted, making her sound like a scared teenager.

"Curt let me come upstairs," she said breathlessly. "I was covering the emergency landing at the airport, and I heard everything over the scanner, so, since I was out they wanted me to come here and I kind of, sort of, felt sleepy and I thought I would lay down for a few minutes and wait for you because I did want to interview you for my story." Regaining her strength, Claire announced, "And, my editor wants me to handle the story from now on." Oh my goodness, rambling, really? she thought as she shifted in her stilettos.

Lance was not happy. His broad shoulders were tight, almost distorting his muscular torso. He had his hands clenched tight to his sides, and a frown marred his handsome face. The light caught his dark hair, but that was nothing compared to the angry flash of those green eyes.

"Why don't you go back to doing your feature stories at the zoo, or wherever you get those stories, and leave the crime beat to Val?"

"Oh, so now it's Val not Valerie," Claire said a little too loud. "Since when did you two get so cozy?"

Claire heard the stories about Valerie at the television station.

The gossip was that if Valerie wanted a man she would stop at nothing to get him, even if he was married with children. Valerie shattered lives and didn't care—no matter whom she hurt. Claire was furious.

"What do you care?" Lance pointedly asked Claire, angry about everything that was transpiring between them.

On the verge of crying, Claire's face turned red thinking about Valerie touching Lance.

"Children, children, I can hear you fighting all the way down the hall, and so can everyone else in this building," Reid said casually as he strolled into Lance's office, finding the two of them staring at each other, trying to gain control of their emotions.

"You guys need to calm down," Reid said as he walked toward Claire, taking her in his arms.

It felt safe to Claire to stand there with Reid holding her, giving her a few moments to gain her composure.

"You look great, Claire. I've missed seeing you."

"I've missed you too, Reid," Claire said softly. Reid turned, one arm still around Claire as if he was protecting *her*.

"Lance, I came in to tell you the Chief wants a quick rundown this morning."

Looking straight at Lance, "You two need to chill and talk. Claire, I'll see you around," he said, kissing her on the cheek before walking out of the room and closing the door behind him.

Reid was the only person Lance had ever confided in about Claire. No one knew about their passionate love affair that abruptly ended before it had a chance to blossom and grow.

As Reid walked down the hall to his office, he reflected back to when it all started for Claire and Lance.

CHAPTER TWO

Six months earlier, prosecutors, defense attorneys, police, witnesses and the media were all in Houston for the capital murder trial of Johnny Watson, a killer who gained national notoriety because of the news reports on the gruesome details of how his victims died, along with Watson's daily outrageous antics in the courtroom.

Watson's trial had been transferred from Dallas to Houston because the judge ruled he couldn't get a fair trial in Dallas.

Every day it was an emotionally charged atmosphere, especially with the victims' families in the courtroom.

The murder investigation and trial consumed Lance and Reid's lives for close to a year. Claire reported on the murder investigation from the beginning.

Through her television news reports, she'd gained the reputation as a cool, calm, no-nonsense type of reporter. The viewers loved her.

The television station was overwhelmed by the positive e-mail and Facebook comments and tweets as well as comments on the station's website, and even phone calls came in about Claire's reporting on the trial.

Sadly, because of the national media portrayal, the crime cast a dark shadow on the Dallas community.

Reid would catch Lance watching Claire throughout the

trial. He recognized the look and knew what Lance wanted. Reid had secretly imagined himself with Claire until he realized how his best friend felt about her.

Lance wanted Claire.

The jury convicted Watson for the murders of two Dallas women. The prosecution held back on presenting evidence on the other murder cases because it was circumstantial.

Lance and Reid quietly feared Watson would go free. After two more days of emotionally draining testimony by family and friends, the jury sentenced Watson to death by lethal injection.

In a chilling moment, Watson turned, framed his evil smile and thanked the jury for their decision before breaking out in a spine-tingling laugh while deputies carried him out of the courtroom.

The whole scene reminded Claire of the Joker's portrayal in the *Batman Beyond* movie.

The trial exhausted everyone. No one would forget the look on the faces of the murdered women's families as the final verdict had been read.

Claire felt sick to her stomach throughout the testimony, especially when family members and friends took the stand, describing the lives of each young woman. They were blonde, brunette, short, tall, successful and smart. A couple of the victims attended the local college, they volunteered in their community, belonged to local churches and had a vision of what they wanted to do and accomplish in their lives.

Many family members ended their testimony condemning Watson, who sat there and smiled throughout the trial.

The last person to testify in the punishment phase of the trial was Barbara Latham, Jenny's mother. Jenny was the last woman murdered before police finally arrested Watson.

Many believed it was the testimony surrounding Jenny's murder and the fact that there were eyewitnesses who saw

Jenny with Watson at dinner the night she was murdered that led to his conviction.

Cool and detached in the beginning, she spoke about Jenny fulfilling her dream of becoming a fashion designer, and the more she spoke of her daughter, her voice quivered until she broke down, shrieking over her Jenny's horrible demise.

Tears streamed down Claire's face. Like everyone in the courtroom, Claire wondered how someone could commit such a gruesome crime on another human being, inflicting such horrific pain. What also made Claire sick was that she understood what the women saw in Watson, with his "bad boy" devilish look, coal black hair he pulled back into a small ponytail and penetrating brown eyes. She understood how the victims were attracted to his muscular body and swagger, and how they easily left with him. Never knowing when they left with him that their fate had been sealed. Watson was rich; he looked it and he acted like it, always assuming he didn't have to play by the rules.

She shivered.

Watson adamantly maintained his innocence throughout the trial. He'd testified in his own defense, staunchly vowing he did not kill Jenny Latham or any other woman. Watson did testify that he had dinner with Jenny the night of her murder. He also testified that he dropped her off at her home and went on his way. His arrogant attitude did him in.

The jury didn't believe Watson was innocent. Watson testified about trying to find Jenny's friend that night, but he never did.

What destroyed Watson's defense was testimony from four women he had dated.

One by one they tearfully told the jury how Watson raped them when they'd tried to resist him. One woman testified about being in his apartment after drinks and dinner and when she told him to stop, she didn't want to have sex, he violently grabbed her hair and dragged her to his bedroom, forcing her to have sex with him more than once throughout the night. None of the women wanted to come forward to police for fear of what it would do to their careers and their status in the community.

The testimony from the four women and Watson's sinister and cocky attitude, acting like he would go free, sealed his fate as well with the jury, even though the evidence was circumstantial surrounding the other female victims and the alleged assaults were never reported to police, which meant there was no DNA evidence connecting Watson. Investigators did, however, connect Watson with the women on those specific nights through restaurant receipts and eyewitnesses' testimony.

Claire also wondered if the jury wasn't just sick of hearing day in and day out about the murders and just wanted to convict so it would all go away.

Claire turned and looked out through the back window of the courtroom. She saw Lance watching her, concern in his eyes. It was a look only for her. She imagined Lance, strong, strong Lance, taking her in his arms and soothing her fears, although they had never done anything more than talk, or the occasional interview for a story she was working on.

How odd these strong feelings she felt for him.

Lance was beyond feeling any emotion about what was happening inside the courtroom. He endured months and months of anguish discovering the brutally murdered females, leading the investigation until finally arresting Watson.

That night, following the afternoon verdict, there was the traditional "after trial party," at a local hotel. The partygoers included attorneys, police, the media, and anyone else involved in the trial. It was an excuse to "blow off steam" from the stress of the trial and a chance to unwind.

An unspoken rule at these parties, comments and actions were "off the record" by all sides, giving the party a more relaxed atmosphere.

At first, Reid was shocked to see Claire walk up to Lance, touch his arm and congratulate him for his victory.

He and Lance had been standing on the balcony, drinking a beer, looking out at the party festivities below, contemplating if they should join in.

It seemed so intimate, the way Claire touched Lance.

Moments earlier two of the court reporters, Melody James and Sarah Collins, yelled up at Lance and Reid from the courtyard. It was hard to hear them with the music and partying crowd in the background. Melody and Sarah were holding large mugs of beer.

"Hey, detectives, come on down. Let's dance and have some fun," Melody said.

"Detective Sanchez, I need to tell you a secret," Sarah called up, then the two ladies started laughing.

"See you in a minute," Reid called down to them before taking a sip from his beer.

Reid had stepped back when Claire walked up, and now as he glanced over, shock washed over him as Lance pulled Claire into his arms, gently kissing her. Reid knew Lance wasn't going downstairs to join in the party.

Claire did not resist.

It seemed so out of character for Lance to be so gentle, always displaying such a macho and edgy exterior.

When they stopped kissing, Lance took Claire's hand and they casually left the balcony and Reid alone with his thoughts.

Lance called Reid on his cell phone an hour later.

"Hey, I'm going to the beach house, I'll see you in a couple of days."

Lance's beach house was forty minutes away from Houston on the Texas Gulf Coast in Galveston. Lance's grandparents left it to him when they died. It was Lance's quiet haven away from the crimes of the world. Now, he was taking the one person he thought he was falling in love with, to see his private escape from life as a detective.

Lance grew up in Dallas' Highland Park with two other brothers, always in competition with each other, playing football and baseball throughout high school. Lance had gone off to the University of Texas at Austin, where he graduated with a business degree.

But things changed while he was at college. His uncle Nathan had gone off to Iraq and then later Afghanistan, where he was in the United States Special Forces.

Growing up, Nathan was always at the their sports games and was always there for them if they needed to talk or just hang out.

Lance's senior year in college he received the call from his father that would change his life forever.

He was on his way to his economics class when his cell phone rang.

"Dad, what's up?"

"Lance, I'm sorry to bother you," his father choked. "It's my brother, your uncle Nate." Then he tearfully cried out, "He's gone, son. Nate was killed in Afghanistan. His body is coming home." Crying more, "Son, I'll let you know when he gets home. I love you," and his dad disconnected the call.

Standing outside of his class in the business building, swarms of students were talking, laughing, moving on to the next class, but Lance couldn't move. As the hallway began to clear and doors closed, Lance stood there.

He didn't know for how long he was frozen there. Then Lance left, went into his house, packed up, and drove home to see his family and mourn the loss of his Uncle Nate.

Lance knew the day he graduated from college he wasn't going into a career in business. The day after Uncle Nathan was buried with full United States Military honors he applied at the Dallas Police Department to become a police officer.

Two years later, Lance was transferred to the Dallas Police Homicide Division.

CHAPTER THREE

His cell phone rang, bringing Reid back from his thoughts of the past.

"Hello. Yes I'm ready for the preliminary report," he replied to Spencer, who he saw earlier at the murder scene. "Give me what you have. I'll get the report to Lance and the Chief. You have her identity?"

Lance and Claire stared intensely at each other, neither one making a move since Reid walked out and closed the door. Claire's heart started beating fast.

Lance broke the silence. "I'll work with you and do the interview under one condition, you'll have dinner with me after the late news is over. I'll have some Italian food delivered. Want me to meet you at your place or mine?"

His expression softened, "We need to talk, clear up some misunderstandings."

"Bribing the media can get you into trouble," she casually replied. For the first time, she allowed herself to smile.

"That is a risk I'll take," Lance said, smiling back.

It was at that moment, as they both contemplated what was ahead for them, Valerie knocked and opened Lance's door at the same time.

She stopped, shocked to see Lance and Claire standing there facing each other, but not touching. There was no denying the strong emotional and sexual connection they had.

"Have I interrupted something?" Valerie asked evenly to Claire with an angry look on her face.

Lance's cell phone rang. He walked over to his desk to pick it up as the two women stared at each other.

"What do you have?"

"Lance, it's bad. We've identified the victim," Reid said. "Her father is a prominent banker in town. The Chief wants to go with us to tell him. Wyatt said it's the same MO. He raped her and then strangled her. We're still waiting on the toxicology report."

"I'll be right there."

Hanging the phone up, Lance picked up his coffee cup and tried to appear lighthearted as he walked towards the door.

"Ladies, I have work to do," turning around on his way out the door, "Claire, Corporal Mays will be in touch. I'll meet you downstairs in front of the police station in time for the live news interview tonight." He gave a slight smile and then he was gone.

Claire knew Lance well enough to know it was not good news he had heard on the phone. Claire knew his body language, and it told a different story.

"I'm asking you again. What was that all about?"

Ignoring Valerie, Claire looked out the doorway and glass office windows, her eyes following Lance down the hallway. Claire shivered, feeling there was something evil happening and praying Lance could stop it.

CHAPTER FOUR

Johnny sat on the edge of his bed, looking down at the package he had just received. It was just a matter of time before the prison guards would come get him and take him to his job of cleaning the kitchen.

It had been a little over six months since he walked through the gates of the Huntsville State Prison, home to the Ellis Unit, and some of the most dangerous criminals in the world. Johnny didn't consider himself one of them.

Because of his size he had fought off the first attack made on him, so most of the other inmates left him alone. At six foot three, weighing 250 pounds with the body of a linebacker, Johnny was able to keep to himself and not worry about becoming someone's plaything.

Johnny was not guilty of killing those women. His hot temper had landed him in prison. The jury couldn't see past the women who testified that he had raped them. What do they expect when they tease a man?

Johnny came from a rich family. His father made his name in the real estate and development business, and after the death of his parents he had taken over the company.

MW Resources left him and his twin brother, Clark, a hefty inheritance that allowed him to do what he wanted, anytime, anywhere.

Johnny could feel his anger starting to take hold when he thought of his jackass attorney, who he paid a lot of money to defend him. He wanted to kill his attorney, who at this hour was filing appeal after appeal to get Johnny a new trial.

Most recently, his conviction was upheld in the appeals court, but Johnny knew any day now he would hear good news.

Johnny's attitude during the first trial didn't help much either. He had sneered at witnesses and was prone to several outbursts during the trial that he realized didn't help his situation. He knew he would have to work on holding his temper.

Johnny made the mistake of having a date with one of the victims, Jenny something. He couldn't really remember her name. After dinner, Johnny thought sex was certain until she turned him down flat. He left and someone else came to her house and killed her.

For once he held his temper and let her go, the last one to see her walk into her condo. What a shame, he thought. She had looked good. He had tried to call Jenny's friend, who he knew would let him in, but she'd never answered her cell phone, so he went home. Two days later he was arrested by detectives and charged with capital murder for Jenny's murder. His parents' connections gave him the opportunity to get bail, despite outcries from the community. Screw them.

He remembered seeing Jeremy talking to Jenny in the bar and had nearly thrown a punch at him. Johnny had wanted his attorney to call Jeremy as a witness, but Jeremy had threatened him. Jeremy told him the photographs he was providing Johnny of the news reporter, Claire McKenzie, would stop and he would share with the prosecutors about them.

"Yeah, call me as a defense witness and I'll tell them everything about your obsession with that news anchor and how you have thousands of photographs of her," Jeremy sneered.

"That'll look good to the jury."

Months earlier they had met at the Hooters bar off of Greenville Avenue. Johnny had told his attorney he was going to ask Jeremy for help with his case. They weren't best friends, but he didn't expect this anger from Jeremy.

"That would really help your case. You leave me out of your pissing problem, or I'll help do you in." The guy pushed back his bar stool and walked out. Johnny later told his attorney to forget it. He knew it could hurt his case if Jeremy did what he was threatening to do.

Johnny thought back to when he had met Jeremy. It happened at The Rio Club, a nightclub in Dallas. They struck up a conversation when Johnny was ordering a drink.

"Hey, how is it tonight?" Johnny asked.

"I see a few," Jeremy replied. "What do you do?"

"Real estate. What about you?"

"Photography."

"Hey, you ever been out on business and seen that Claire McKenzie? Now that's a great piece. Do you know her?"

"I've seen her around."

And that's how it started. Usually, once a month they would meet at different nightclubs, competing over who left the club with a lady first.

Johnny could tell Jeremy had an angry streak. One time he walked out of a nightclub to see Jeremy in the parking lot, yelling at a young woman next to his Tahoe. He was waving his arms up and down, jerking around. That even made Johnny nervous, and that was hard to do. Finally, and thankfully, they'd jumped in the Tahoe and drove away. Johnny had not wanted to get in the middle of it, and he was moments away from doing that. Six months after meeting Jeremy, Johnny mustered enough nerve to ask about Claire again.

"Hey, you have any extra photographs of that Claire chick?"

"You want some for your own personal stash? It'll cost you, and any other women I take photographs of," Jeremy had said, laughing.

"I have the money."

It did cost Johnny several thousand dollars twice a year.

A week later the first photograph of Claire arrived at Johnny's office.

He couldn't believe his eyes. Claire was bent over, picking up a notebook. He could see her red thong under her skirt. Johnny closed his eyes, recalling the memory of that first photograph. Then, other photographs started coming in of various women around the Dallas social scene. The only thing that kept him from losing his mind in this prison hell hole was the fact that Clark, his younger, idiot brother, was coming to see him next week and his plan would kick in.

Money talked.

Through his attorney, Johnny already paid fifty thousand dollars to a prison guard who was going to turn the other way when his brother arrived. That's when he was going to make the switch with his twin brother. He had a stash of drugs he was going to give his brother and then walk out of prison as Clark Watson, a free man. By the time his idiot twin brother woke up and started screaming about who he was, Johnny would be long gone.

What a stupid idiot his brother was. Clark had always been scared of Johnny growing up because of the treacherous acts Johnny committed against him, losing his temper and hitting his brother in the head with a golf club, putting dead animals in his bed. He'd terrorized his brother for years, and when Clark left home for college he never returned. It traumatized his mother, who flew to Washington DC on a regular basis to see Clark. Clark vowed never to return to Dallas, and once again, with the help of several thousand dollars, Clark kept his promise and stayed away.

He had been paid off by Johnny never to reveal why, and that left Johnny with the chance to take over the family business. He was smarter than Clark anyway, who lived high and mighty off of his inheritance. But through Johnny's private investigator, he discovered that Clark had made some bad investments and was going through money faster than water coming out of a faucet.

That was the only reason why his brother was coming here to the state prison to see him, even though he despised his very existence. The wheels of his plan were in motion, and Johnny would be kissing the air of freedom in a matter of days.

Suddenly, the trap door of his cell opened, and a newspaper was thrown inside, another perk money bought.

"Hey, Watson, here's your morning glory, asshole," the guard said, laughing as he latched the trap door shut.

"Hey, kiss my ass," Johnny yelled.

He stared at the Dallas Morning News newspaper strewn along the floor and he couldn't believe what he saw. The front page showed a picture of Detective Lance Harris, kneeling down over a dead female body.

The headlines screamed at him: "The Smiley Face Serial Killer is Loose." "Woman found murdered in the park."

Shaking, Johnny leaned over to pick up the newspaper.

CHAPTER FIVE

Lance intercepted Reid outside the Chief's office door.

"What do you have?"

His partner looked down at his notebook, "Jessica Campbell, the daughter of Ann Lorraine and Brandon Campbell, a prominent banker in Dallas. She was last seen at the Dixie Club, that new hotspot. Ryan got in touch with the owner. He had the bartenders come in for an interview. One of them remembered her. He thinks he may have seen her leave with someone. The witness described a tall dark guy, muscular, but he didn't see his face and can't remember the hair color."

"He must have been watching her."

"Wonder what he had in mind?"

"We need to be there tonight to interview patrons who might have seen Jessica or this guy she supposedly left with."

"Officer Belinski, the police clergy and his assistant, Officer Madison, left an hour ago to tell the Campbells. They are expecting us at any time."

Suddenly, the Chief's door opened and Preston Pierce, the Police Communications Officer and the Chief's errand boy stood there.

"Detectives, the Chief will see you now," Pierce said as he waved them in.

Lance walked in first with Reid behind him.

Chief Lewis looked up from his desk. He didn't stand or offer to shake their hands.

"I know what you have, and it's not much," he said.

Lance didn't reply. He was waiting for the Chief to finish his tirade.

"I know the Campbells, and they are devastated. They want to know why our hotshot detective division can't find this killer."

"We may have a witness, sir, maybe more. We won't know until tonight when we go to the Dixie Club and conduct interviews." Lance tried to keep his calm. He didn't want to take the bait from the Chief and end up in a shouting match, a scene that had happened before.

Reid began to fill their boss in on what they knew while Lance looked straight at him, no expression on his face, even though the Chief glared back.

Lance checked out for a moment, not wanting to listen to the Chief's rambling. There had been a falling out between Lance and Chief Lewis a year ago, before the Watson capital murder trial. It was over a woman, Tiffany Swan, a Dallas socialite who badly wanted to get married and was on the prowl.

Tiffany fit the shark female profile perfectly. She was five-four, had a perfectly sculpted figure with double d-sized breasts, thanks to her plastic surgeon, long blonde hair that fell down to the top of her buttocks and blue eyes.

Lance still chided himself for his stupid decision. He'd been late leaving the office and decided to stop in at Mario's to pick up some Mexican food before he went home. He ordered a beer from the bar while he waited. There he ran into Ryan and two other detectives. One beer led to two, another, then he turned and looked into the most beautiful face he had seen in a long time. Tiffany shot her dazzling white smile at him, and before he knew it, she'd joined them at the bar.

She'd put her hand on Lance's thigh under the table. After dinner, the two of them left Mario's together.

Tiffany wasn't someone you resisted. On the way to her place in the Uber ride, she wouldn't keep her hands off of Lance. They'd tumbled into bed. Lance left as soon as Tiffany was asleep, leaving her a note on her bedside dresser. Once he'd sobered up early the next morning he knew trouble... and she was trouble.

Tiffany called the police station the next day and left a breathless message.

"Lance, Sugar, I can't wait until tonight," she said on Lance's voicemail about how she wanted a repeat of last night. Lance had done his best to be unavailable, but two nights later Tiffany showed up on his doorstep.

The doorbell rang.

Lance had fallen asleep on his couch. It was close to midnight. "Who the hell could that be?" he grumbled as he dragged himself off the couch, walking toward the front door.

When he opened the door and saw Tiffany, he could tell immediately she had been drinking.

"Hi there, Handsome," she said as she strolled into Lance's house, uninvited.

But that didn't matter, nobody turned down Tiffany Swan.

"What are you doing here?"

"I came for you Sugar," she said as she turned, a pouty look on her face, and she slightly squeezed her arms together, revealing a bulging cleavage that would send any man into orbit.

"This isn't a good idea."

"Of course it is," she walked up to him and rubbed her breasts against him. "We're perfect together. I'll remind you." She then thrust her body at him.

Lance grabbed Tiffany's arm and pushed her back so he could look at her.

"I'm not looking for a serious relationship right now."

"What do you mean? I thought you liked us together. What's your problem? I have ways to change your mind."

"It's not you. It's me. I just got out of a serious relationship, and I'm not ready to get involved just yet."

"What are you trying to tell me?" Tiffany asked. Lance could sense her anger rising.

"You're a beautiful, smart young woman, but right now I'm not the man that can be committed to you."

"Oh I get it, screw me and add me to your belt notch. Did you enjoy telling your cop buddies? You really are into yourself, aren't you, Mr. Detective Harris?"

"Tiffany, I'm sorry."

She attempted to swing at Lance, who caught it in mid-air.

"That wouldn't be a smart thing to do, Tiffany," Lance pulled her arm down to her side. "You have been drinking—let me call you a cab." He looked around for his cell phone.

"Oh, going to take me in like the hotshot detective you think you are? Well, screw you. I'm out of here."

In a huff, Tiffany turned and walked out the front door, slamming it behind her.

Lance stood there for a moment. That hadn't gone well, but he couldn't let it go any further. He could see trouble written all over that chick. Who was he kidding? He couldn't be with anyone but Claire, and he really screwed that up.

He hoped Tiffany made it home safely.

He felt she had enough anger shooting through her veins to ward off the alcohol effect.

Lance turned and walked into his kitchen. It was a modern kitchen with a masculine feel with wood floors, white walls, dark wood paneling and stainless steel appliances.

Oh, hell, Lance thought, as he grabbed his keys off the counter. He had to make sure Tiffany made it home. He turned back around and opened his desk drawer where he had put her address from the other night. Grabbing the piece of paper and reading the address, he realized she only lived about ten blocks from him.

Jogging out to his truck, Lance jumped in and started the motor up, heading fast down the street. Moments later he pulled up next to Tiffany's house. Her blue Escalade was parked out front. He turned his truck around and headed home.

CHAPTER SIX

"At least have the decency to listen to your commander," Lewis shouted, glaring at Lance, jerking him out of his past thoughts. "What else are you doing to find this killer? It doesn't sound like you have anything."

"Sir, we're going to the Campbells' this afternoon to give our condolences, but we're also hoping that they'll let us look in their daughter's room. We're going to reconstruct the last three days of her life, check out her boyfriend and past boyfriends. We need to know everyone she came in contact with."

"That doesn't sound like much, but it's a start."

"Chief, we'd like to issue a warning that we might have a serial killer out there."

"Are you crazy? Do you know what that will do to our tourism and conventions?" Lewis said, appearing baffled by Lance's request. "If you were doing your job we wouldn't even be here having this conversation."

Lance turned to Reid, then back to the Chief.

"We need to get going."

Lance and Reid started to walk out, knowing they were dismissed. The Communications Director had remained quiet throughout the exchange.

"Harris, you need to leave the media interviews to me."

Lance nearly smacked Preston in the face.

The guy was such an egomaniac.

Lance did everything he could to stay away from the media.

Lance knew Reid couldn't stand Pierce either, because he enjoyed seeing himself on television and didn't really care if the criminal was behind bars.

"Pierce, I'm a deputy chief and don't you forget it," Lance said, pointing his finger at Pierce, trying not to lose his temper.

Turning his attention back to Chief Lewis, "Sir, would you like to join us and go to the Campbell's? We're on our way now, and I was told earlier you wanted to go."

"No, go ahead. I'm tied up here," Lewis said, surprising the two veteran cops, knowing that Lewis was also a media hound, always wanting to have his name and face plastered everywhere. What a perfect opportunity for the Chief to get Internet, newspaper and television coverage. It shocked Lance. What was going on?

Lance looked at Pierce as he and Reid attempted to leave.

"You can release the name of the victim in two hours. That will give us time to get over to the Campbell's, talk to them and gather evidence."

Lance and Reid exited the Chief's office as the door slammed shut behind them.

They could hear Pierce shouting about Harris and how he didn't have the right to tell him how to handle the media.

"We might as well head over to the Campbell's house," Lance somberly said to Reid.

"I'll never get over the pain of having to go talk to a family when a loved one has been murdered, especially a daughter or son," Reid replied.

"Yeah, it sucks."

The spring temperature and humidity slapped Lance in the face as they exited the police station out the back door in an attempt to slip by the media.

The weather was warm but still outside, no hint that rain would be coming anytime soon. Lance and his partner jumped into Lance's black Ford truck. His truck was his pride and joy. Lance bought it with the inheritance money his grandparents left. Paid cash.

"I'm going to nail this bastard," Lance said as he started his high-powered engine, pulled out of the police parking lot and hit the gas.

The two drove in silence.

Lance was going over details of the investigation in his mind, and he had no doubt that Reid's lack of conversation meant he was too.

Lance pulled up in front of a great white mansion, old and elegant, with white brick, a wraparound porch and shutters painted a dark green. The Campbell home was located in historic University Park. A perfect house where a perfect family once lived, now shattered by a killer.

"You ready?" he asked.

"Never, but let's do it."

Lance and Reid opened the truck doors, slowly getting out and walking toward the front porch steps. Getting up to the house seemed to take forever. Ringing the doorbell, the two detectives waited.

A man answered who Lance recognized as Brandon Campbell from newspaper articles he'd read in the past about Campbell, who was a robust man, close to his late fifties, Lance guessed.

Reaching out his hand, Lance said, "Mr. Campbell, Chief Deputy Lance Harris. I want to tell you how sorry we are about your daughter."

"Just catch the bastard who did this. Please come in," Campbell said, remembering his manners despite his grief, motioning for the two detectives to come inside.

"We can talk in the great room."

They walked into a spacious room, with long red velvet curtains and dark brown leather furniture. It had a high-powered feel to it, like many deals had been cut, decided and finalized in this very room, with nothing more than a hand shake.

After they were all seated, Lance and Reid in two leather chairs, while Campbell sat down on the couch, reaching out to get what appeared to be a scotch and water.

"I'll send for Ann in a moment. She is heavily sedated so I'm not sure how much she can tell you. I'm devastated over Jessica. My wife appears to be in a coma, and I'm not sure what to do right now," Campbell said in a shaky voice.

Lance and Reid noticed that Campbell seemed unsteady on his feet and his mind seemed to wonder, but it was under-standable, his daughter had been murdered. His life was destroyed.

"What can you tell us about the last time you saw your daughter, Mr. Campbell?" Lance asked as he reached in his pocket for his notebook.

"She came home from getting her hair cut, and she seemed happy and excited. You know how it is at that age, nothing can go wrong." Campbell sighed, looking down at his drink, obviously remembering. The phone rang and the doorbell bellowed a long ring tone at the same time.

Campbell stood up and started walking towards the front door. "Excuse me for a moment."

Lance and Reid watched as their victim's father met an elderly, frumpy looking woman in the foyer. She was dressed in black. He gave her instructions that the detectives couldn't hear.

Campbell walked back to the great room, still carrying his drink, not taking a sip yet. He sat down again on the couch, resting his drink down on a coaster on the table.

"Rosalind, our housekeeper, will take care of the phone and door until we finish. I've instructed her not to disturb us."

"Please continue, Mr. Campbell. Did Jessica let on to why she was excited or what plans she might have had?" Reid asked.

"She was going to a nightclub with some girlfriends and then she said she was going to meet Brad later."

"But she never met Brad," a voice boomed down the stairs. As the three looked in the direction of the sound. A tall, thin, elegantly dressed woman in beige pants and a starched white shirt slowly walked down the stairs, wearing high heeled beige sandals that clicked on the marble stairs as she descended.

Ann Lorraine Campbell.

If it had not been for the horrific reason for the two detectives to be in this beautiful home, Lance imagined she had descended those stairs in the same aristocratic fashion many times over the years.

He noted immediately where Jessica got her beauty from.

Ann Campbell, despite her thirty-year difference, was breathtakingly beautiful with blonde hair tied in a bun behind her neck, a slender neck, and despite some wrinkles around the eyes and lips, she had striking green eyes, just like her daughter once had.

Brandon Campbell immediately jumped up and walked toward his wife. He took her in his arms and they stood there for a moment surrounded in their grief. Campbell whispered something to Ann and she shook her head then led the way back into the great room.

She reached out her hand toward the detectives. Lance took her hand in his.

"I am so sorry," Lance said.

"Thank you. I'm on medication, so if I stop in thought, please give me a moment."

"Certainly."

Reid stood next and took her hands in his. "On behalf of the Dallas Police Department, please know we are doing everything we can to find who did this,"

Jessica's name was left unspoken for the moment.

Ann made no attempt to remove her hands from Reid. It was as if she was holding on for her life.

Lance spoke up as Ann turned and looked up at him, as if noticing him for the first time. "Mrs. Campbell, you mentioned a moment ago that Brad, I'm assuming was Jessica's boyfriend, didn't catch up with her last night."

"Yes, that's right. I talked to Brad's mother, Stephanie Yeager, a couple of hours ago after the first officers came to tell us and she said Brad didn't see Jessica, that he was told she'd already left."

"Mrs. Campbell, we're going to need contact information for Brad and his mother," Lance said.

"Yes, of course, Detective. I'll get you everything," Mr. Campbell replied where he was sitting on the couch.

Lance continued, "Did this Brad Yeager say who told him Jessica had left and with whom?"

"No, I had the impression Brad may have been upset with Jessica for leaving, but now..." Ann's voice trailed off and the tears began to roll down her cheeks. Campbell jumped up from the couch and held his wife again. Both were crying.

Lance and Reid remained quiet. The anger welled up inside of Lance, seeing the grief, devastation and collapse of a family at the hands of scum.

Ann turned to face Lance.

"It is so unlike Jessica to leave with someone she doesn't know. She was a wonderful child. All she wanted was to be a broadcast journalist. Jessica interviewed with Channel Two to do a summer internship at the television station and it was set to start on June 15."

Lance and Reid looked at each other. New information.

Lance could tell Ann was getting ready to lose her calm.

"Why, Detective, why?" Ann shrieked before collapsing to the ground, Brandon trying to pull her up. Lance helped and the two parents slowly walked to the front foyer stairs that Lance assumed led up to their master bedroom. Lance and Reid stood as the Campbells slowly went up the stairs.

"I hope the son-of-a-bitch gives me every opportunity to kill him when we get him," Reid said with clinched teeth. Lance didn't answer. It was times like this when Lance didn't believe that the guilty deserved justice. No, they deserved to die.

Five minutes later, Brandon Campbell returned to the great room. This time he picked up his drink and drained it. He stepped over to his bar and refilled it again. This time with straight scotch, no water.

"I'm sorry. We still can't believe that Jessica isn't going to come flying through the door, purse and shopping bags, ready to tell us the latest story she had uncovered. You did know that she was going to college to become a journalist, a television journalist? Her professor had told her she had great promise and a great voice," Campbell's voice trailed off. "She was looking forward to working with Claire McKenzie, that reporter at Channel Two. She seems so talented."

Lance stopped for a moment.

Surely, there was no connection.

"Sir, I hate to ask you this, but could we look through Jessica's room? We'd also like to take her computer with us. Do you know if she had a Facebook page or a website?"

"Whatever any of the other kids had going, I'm sure Jessica did. We always talked to her about the dangers of meeting anyone in person that she talked to online."

Brandon's eyes grew wide. "You don't think she met someone from a chat room or something, one of those sexual predators?"

"We don't know, sir, but it is something we need to look at," Lance replied.

"Come this way. Jessica moved her bedroom downstairs last year before she left for college. Said she wanted to have more privacy."

Brandon shuffled down the hall. Part of the effects from the alcohol and from the devastation of losing his only child.

Lance and Reid knew the family had a long road to recovery, if they ever did recover from losing Jessica.

Campbell opened the door to a spacious room with a king-sized bed and a decorative fuchsia, lime green and purple bedspread.

There was a desk in the right corner with a computer on top, and it looked to Lance, equipped with all the latest electronic technology. A stereo system sat in a built-in cabinet next to the computer and desk.

The room was wide and airy, with white walls and paneling, but loads of color in the bedspread, curtains and pillows that were lined up on the bed. A purple lounge chair faced out on towards the backyard where the room opened out onto a patio that led down to the swimming pool.

It was beautiful.

Jessica's bed was made and the room was straight. Photographs of family and friends lined the wall that led to the bathroom. One picture after another of a smiling, beautiful Jessica Campbell, whose lifeless body now lay on a slab in the Dallas County morgue, awaiting an autopsy.

The screen on her computer had a light flashing, notifying her that she'd received a new e-mail. On the desk there were books on journalism, and stacked up on top was a book by television news personality Diane Sawyer.

"Do you mind if I call in the crime scene investigator team and lab technicians, Mr. Campbell?" Lance asked.

"Do what you need to do. I'll be in my study. I have several phone calls that need to be made, and I'll get that contact information for you." Campbell left the detectives standing in the middle of the bedroom. Lance pulled his phone clip off his belt and used his cell to call in the forensics squad.

"Be sure and bring that computer nerd Jacob," Lance told lead crime scene investigator Jerry Sikes, the head of the Dallas evidence team. "I think this computer holds the key to what happened."

Lance ended his call.

"Let's have a look around."

CHAPTER SEVEN

Back in the Channel Two television station newsroom on her computer, Claire finished writing the lead to her 5pm news story. With the press of a button on her computer, the intro would be immediately transferred to the news anchor teleprompter in time for the newscast.

There was a low roar inside the newsroom.

It was Claire's favorite time of day, even though it was always hectic with people on their computers, running into editing to finish up their story, on the phone with sources, and the producer and news director marching around letting everyone know their jobs were on the line if they didn't make deadline. No one was ever fired, but it was tradition for this scenario to take place.

The sounds of editing machines spinning, computer keys tapping and voices speaking as the newsroom prepared for the 5pm and 6pm newscasts coming up in an hour.

The background noise of the newsroom was a comforting sound to Claire, computers tapping, editing machines whizzing, people on the phone, always testing each other to be the best.

It gave way to an excitement of anticipation in the air, and it was thrilling to Claire to be a part of something historical every night.

Staring at her computer, deep in thought, and praying for

the right words to lead in to her live interview with Lance on the 6pm news, Claire jumped when Chandler came up behind her, putting his arms loosely around her neck in his usual bear hug.

She shrieked as several news reporters and one of the main anchors, Dwight Hall, turned to see what was going on. When they noticed it was Chandler everyone returned to what they were doing.

"Hey girl, why are you so jumpy?" Chandler asked as he released his arms and spun her chair around so she could face him.

He sat down in the chair that was behind Claire, facing her and putting his hands on the top of her legs.

"Chandler, you turd, you scared the living daylights out of me," Claire said, annoyed as she playfully pushed his shoulder. He was always touching her. It was like an ownership.

Claire had been grateful in the beginning when he had attached himself to her, letting everyone know he was her exclusive photographer.

It had been comforting since she was the new kid on the block, as they say, and needed to learn the ropes.

Secretly, in the beginning, Claire had enjoyed the attention from Chandler. They'd tried to hook up once in Houston during the Watson capital murder trial. Claire and Chandler had gone out for drinks and dinner one night after a long day in the courtroom at the beginning of the trial.

There was no doubt Chandler was sexy at over six feet tall, muscular and lean from not only working out but from carrying the camera equipment around, and she knew several of the women in the newsroom wished for a chance with him.

Claire had invited Chandler into her room. They'd kissed and he started unbuttoning her blouse.

It didn't feel right to her, but she thought if she could just relax. While it felt soothing to have someone desire you as much as she knew Chandler did, there wasn't that anticipating thrill or excitement to keep going.

Claire pulled back.

"Chandler, you are my best friend and I can't do this," she told Chandler as she pulled away and buttoned her blouse.

"Baby, what's wrong?" Chandler said as he tried to embrace Claire again.

She used every ounce of strength she had not to grimace.

"I don't want to lose what we have, and I don't think I'm ready for this right now." She hoped Chandler wouldn't get upset or offended and would just leave her room.

"It's fine, Claire. Don't worry about it," Chandler said as he pulled her to his chest and hugged her.

Claire had been relieved Chandler had taken it so well. They resumed their friendship-type relationship as though nothing had happened, even though Claire was conscious of what had happened. Penetrating her with his dark blue eyes like he knew what she was always thinking. Claire constantly felt a lustful look from Chandler, but shrugged it off since he never said another word about what happened that night.

Then Lance had entered her life a week later.

Why did it bother her that Chandler was touching her today? It aggravated her for some reason.

"Are you afraid of something? You seem like your mind is somewhere else. Why are you afraid?"

"Chandler, I'm just tired, PMS and the whole nine-yards."

"Don't worry, it's Chandler to the rescue. I've edited your story insert, and it's on its way to the lineup now. I'm going to leave early and set up for your live shot at five. I bet there are going to be loads of newsies out there because of the murder, and I want a nice shaded spot in this horrible heat."

Control. That was what Chandler was all about.

Chandler stood up and started to massage Claire's neck. Something he had done so many times before, but today Claire pulled away.

Chandler could feel his anger swelling inside and took a deep breath to contain it.

"What the hell is up?"

"Chandler, not now. I need to finish my lead for the live shot at six and get my head together. Don't forget I'm doing a live interview with Detective Harris for the six newscast. We'll have to leave the murder scene immediately to get to the police station. Melissa is also trying to set up interviews with Jessica Campbell's friends."

For some reason she could sense that Chandler was angry about that and she wondered why.

"Great, the asshole detective."

"Why do you not like him?"

"Because, Claire, remember what he did to you?"

"So he didn't tell me about having a wife. I did find out later he was going through a divorce, so he told me the truth. He was separated at the time, just like he said."

"If that's the case and he didn't hurt you, then why didn't you call him back? Why didn't he call you? It took months for you to get over him. You saw him today, didn't you? Let me tell you, I've heard the story about Harris and the police Chief's wife, and it's not a pretty picture. He is an asshole."

"Chandler, I don't want to hear about it."

"Great, I'm out of here. Catch a ride with Greg."

Greg was the lead engineer at the news station and a genius at keeping the news equipment up and running. Chandler stormed out of Claire's office, leaving her speechless.

Hillary walked up.

"What's that all about?" Hillary asked Claire as she leaned over the office divider wall.

"I don't get it with him sometimes. He hates Detective Harris and it shouldn't matter."

"Claire, everyone knows Chandler has a temper and he is

madly in love with you. The way you take up for him puts everyone on guard. You need to be careful. I heard him with Valerie the other day. He had her pinned up against the wall yelling at her and scaring the living daylights out of her."

"I've never seen Chandler like that. And consider the source. Valerie makes everyone crazy," Claire replied as she looked back at her computer screen.

"Whatever you say, but I would be careful," Hillary added as she walked to her desk that sat in the middle of the newsroom.

Hillary was one of the assignment editors and filled in as a producer whenever they needed her.

Claire admired her tenacious spirit and determination to get a story. Claire laughed every time she heard Hillary telling the new reporters her "You are lucky to be here now" speech and that "there was never a bad story, just a bad reporter not doing his or her job and getting the story."

The best line was, "Remember, if it bleeds it leads," scaring the new, young news reporters to death. That part of Hillary's speech was buried in the back of Claire's mind. Claire respected Hillary, and her warning Claire about Chandler made her uneasy.

Was there something about Chandler she was blind about?

Better call Greg and let him know I'll need a ride, Claire thought to herself as she leaned across her desk and picked up the phone.

"Greg, what are you doing? What's all that noise behind you?"

"I'm rocking out to the latest Red Hot Chili Peppers song."

Greg was the resident newsroom rock-n-roll fanatic and was trying to get a band together in hopes of making it big in the music industry someday. He talked incessantly about trying out for American Idol.

For now Greg worked as a television engineer, trouble

shooting for computers, cameras and news equipment and shooting a live shot now and then. Claire liked Greg and admired his ambition. Even though he was at least ten years older than Claire, he still had his dreams and Claire hoped this burly, bearded faced, brown haired guy would someday accomplish it.

"What are you up to dollface?"

"I'm trying to finish my lead into my package that will run before my live interview with Detective Harris at six." Claire said as she looked out in the oasis of the newsroom.

"You're interviewing Harris? Great guy and solid. Okay, I didn't know we had an interview, but no problem."

"I also have a live shot at five. Chandler already left to go to the murder scene for the early news where we are going live."

"Let's leave soon to be ready."

"Chandler will be there waiting."

"Now there's a guy that is too intense. See you out back."

Another observation about Chandler. What was it she didn't see?

Claire looked down at her watch. She had fifteen minutes.

"Great, I'll see you downstairs by your truck," Claire said as she hung up the phone.

Claire knew she needed to hurry, but she was distracted once again about Chandler.

What was the deal with him? She felt that uneasy, woman's intuition creeping in. Why Greg liked Lance and Chandler didn't.

"Too many M's for moody men in my life," Claire said out loud to no one in particular. "I thought women were supposed to be the drama queens."

Claire would just have to wing it for her intro to her live shot. The words weren't coming. She left it open on the script, hit the button and sent it in. She might find out some new information anyway about the murder investigation. It was good she was going early. Her package would run at five with her live intro and then her revised story that Chandler edited would wrap around her live shot.

At the 6pm news, she had the interview with Lance and then she would worry about the ten newscast later.

She picked up her office phone to call Melissa, one of the newsroom interns helping her out this spring. Melissa was a junior at Southern Methodist University, the local private college.

Melissa answered, and Claire could tell she had food in her mouth by the way she said hello. The girl was always eating something, and yet she was skinny as a rail. It drove Claire crazy. She always had to watch what she ate now that she didn't have the time to do her ballet lessons like she did in college.

"Melissa, what's the latest?"

"I have phone calls out now. I'm trying to get a couple of her friends to meet us for an interview."

"Great. Let me know. I'm on my way to my live shot."

Claire hung up.

She grabbed her cell phone from her desk, scooped up her purse and notepad and headed to makeup. She was going to barely make it on time.

....

Chandler stormed out of the newsroom to his new black Dodge Viper. The camera equipment was already in his car.

He opened the door, jumped in and slammed his fists on the steering wheel as his car door automatically closed.

Claire can be such a selfish bitch sometimes, he thought to himself. But he loved her and would forgive her no matter what.

He attempted to calm himself down, thinking about how he was going to be patient and wait for Claire to realize her feelings towards him. "Patience, the Lord would say." As long as Claire didn't hook up with that jackass detective, everything would be fine between them.

Chandler turned the key and kicked off his powerful engine. As it started, he enjoyed the thrill of hearing it revolve through its cycles.

He craved the sound of the engine, and then turned his radio up full blast after he put his car in reverse and pulled out into the parking lot, shifting into the drive gear and shooting out of the television station parking lot with rap music from Jay Z, playing as loud as it could.

He raced on his way to the scene of the crime.

Lance and Reid walked down the steps of the colonial-style mansion where the Campbells lived. They could hear Mrs. Campbell crying and screaming as Mr. Campbell closed the door behind them.

"We've got to find this bastard."

"I hate to say it, but it's like he knows where we are and is one step ahead," Reid replied.

"I'm going back to the scene. There might be something I missed," Lance said.

"Drop me at the station. I'll check and see if any test results or reports have come in."

"After my interview we'll hit the nightclub. Someone saw her and someone saw our killer, too. I can feel it."

"Are you still going to Huntsville tomorrow to see our favorite serial killer?"

"I don't have a choice. I have this feeling Watson's involved somehow."

Reid nodded as he opened the door.

Lance thought back to after the trial. He had been trying to get over the misery of dealing with his ex-wife and Claire. He had been finished with his ex-wife a long time ago. No bitter feelings. It just didn't work out. Their lust for each other didn't grow into a long-lasting relationship. Lance enjoyed the outdoors—Joann would rather lie on the couch and watch television reruns like *Friends, Seinfeld* or *Sex and the City*.

But he wasn't finished with Claire McKenzie. Tonight would not be the night to try and fix what happened. Lance would be out most of the night, interviewing and searching for this maniac.

As soon as he caught the killer, and he would, Lance made a promise to himself that he would do whatever needed to be done to fix things between him and Claire. If not tonight, someday in the future, soon. He pulled up in the back of the station. Reid jumped out and took off in a jog. Lance turned and looked around. The park was maybe fifteen minutes away, the scene of the crime.

It was four in the afternoon. Claire and Greg were on their way back to the park where the murdered college coed was found early that morning. Claire would do a live shot from the murder scene and then head over to the police department for the six newscast. Chandler already edited two stories that Claire had rewritten with information they had for now. The latest, she would report live.

"Greg, look, there's Detective Harris headed for the taped-off area by the police. I wonder what he's doing?"

"Hopefully his job and he gets this son-of-a bitch soon. I worry about you, Claire, and all the other women when some crazy comes out like this."

"It spooks me too, especially after covering the Watson capital murder trial. Now there's someone who's creepy. Hey, there's Chandler setting up over there by that oak tree."

Greg turned the news van full right to head toward Chandler. The tires screeched a horrible sound and Claire hoped the brakes didn't go out. She would have to remind the guys to get it checked out.

Claire had to hand it to Chandler. He had a great eye for

the visual. He'd managed to set up the camera where Claire would have the crime scene detectives working behind her. He was as close as the police would let him get. There was even an officer standing next to the taped-off crime scene that would only add to the picture, but Claire figured he was also there to make sure they didn't try to move in any closer and try and take pictures.

Greg stopped the truck about ten feet away. Claire jumped out, notebook in hand, and started walking towards Chandler.

"Claire, I'm going to start stringing the cables across," Greg called out to her.

"Thanks, Greg. Yell if you need any help."

As Claire started towards Chandler, he looked up and waved in the opposite direction. That's when she saw several other news reporters standing with the Dallas Police Communications Director, Preston Pierce. She ran over to see what she could find out.

Claire already knew the name of the victim, Jessica Campbell. Melissa had been on the Internet all afternoon pulling up background information on Jessica that she could use in her live report. Even though they both went to SMU, Melissa had said she only met Jessica a couple of times. She left a message at the Campbell's house.

A spokesperson, family friend and attorney, notified the news media that the Campbells would not have any comment today. That was the worst part of her job. Claire despised having to contact the victim's family and those left behind.

Melissa, the intern helping her, was already on the phone making calls to Jessica's friends. She was still in college and although she didn't know Jessica personally, she knew some of her friends. Melissa would try and set up the reaction interviews for her.

Claire's cell phone rang to the music of the country and western band Rascal Flatts as she walked across the asphalt parking lot that connected to the Midtown Park.

This late in the afternoon, the Texas sun continued to bear down, and Claire felt perspiration form on the top of her forehead and lip. Sometimes the heat was unbearable, even though it was only mid-May and only close to summer, the humidity was high. She would have to freshen up her makeup before the news.

Claire flipped open her black RAZR cell phone she had hooked to her straight white skirt.

"Melissa, what's up?"

"Claire, I have it," Melissa excitedly said. "I have it set up for us to meet three of her girlfriends at the Starbucks on Mockingbird Lane just down the street from the Dixie Club."

"That's great, but what's the deal about meeting there?"

"Claire, Jessica was at the Dixie Club last night and left with some guy. That's when she disappeared."

"Oh, my god, I didn't know about the Dixie Club. Maybe we need to go there tonight after we get the interviews edited for the ten newscast. This is starting to look like that case in Aruba where Natalee Holloway disappeared. I think she left with a guy, too. Anyway, thanks Melissa."

"I'll meet you there at 5:15 after our live shot at five. You're only five minutes from there."

Claire ended the call. Her cell rang again and she looked at the number. It was Eric. He had been calling every hour, and Claire was about to explode. He knew she was working on a story and he was being a jerk.

"I've had it with him," she thought as her cell phone rang again. Claire decided to answer it and put an end to what she considered Eric badgering her.

"Hello."

"Claire, what is going on? I've been calling all day."

"Well, if you haven't seen the news or listened to the radio or talked to anybody you would know that another girl has been murdered and I'm working the story."

"Why do they have you on the story? I thought we had plans tonight."

Claire could tell that he was getting angry as she walked across the parking lot to the gathering of reporters off to the side.

Claire felt sick. It was time for this to stop, especially if she was going to talk to Lance. Claire felt afraid of Eric—it didn't feel right and she knew then the reason she didn't completely break it off was because she was afraid of Eric. Even though there was nothing to begin with.

"Eric, I'm covering the story because I'm good and we don't have plans tonight."

"I don't get it, Claire."

"Get this. I have to go to work. We did not have plans tonight. Meet me at Starbucks on Lemmon Avenue at nine tomorrow morning. I've got to go, and don't call me again tonight."

She slammed shut her cell phone and slid it into her pocket skirt holder. She was trying to calm down as she approached the group of news reporters.

Her high heeled sandals were loudly clicking on the asphalt as she walked. Claire was having trouble breathing. She was so furious with Eric and herself for letting it get this far. Claire met Eric at a party a couple of months ago. Her friend, Kathleen, had a summer bash at her parents' posh, Highland Park home with the big backyard and swimming pool. Kathleen had known Eric from graduate school, although they never dated. Eric was getting his graduate degree in business and then he was planning to take over his father's electronics company.

Claire was a little bit interested, but in no way was it love at first sight. They had a couple of dates. She knew it would never go anywhere. While he was fun to be with she had no feelings for him. It was at that point Claire started distancing herself from him.

If Eric noticed the change in her, he never brought it up until a week ago when he tried to kiss her after they had gone to a movie. Claire had stopped the kiss, thanked him for the evening, and turned to go into her house when Eric grabbed her and forced her up against the brick wall, rubbing against her. Claire knew then Eric was trouble. Struggling to get away, Eric apologized, but it didn't matter.

She would never be around Eric again. Her woman's intuition had kicked in, and that was it. All she had to do now was get some computer equipment she had taken to his house one time when she was helping him on a project, and her tennis bag.

As Claire walked up to the impromptu news conference being held by Officer Pierce, Michael Chase, a news reporter from the competing affiliate TV station, turned and gave Claire his usual snide look.

Michael didn't know how close he came to getting socked in the mouth. Claire was sick of men and their manipulation.

She'd scooped Michael a couple of times, and there wasn't a warm feeling between them.

Claire leaned in to listen to Officer Pierce. She already knew she had the latest information, and she wasn't telling anyone, not even Lance, when she interviewed him at six.

Claire knew the Dixie Club, that popular Dallas nightclub, held the answers for her.

Lance had come to the crime scene again where Jessica was found, planning to search the scene.

"What's new, Randy?" Lance asked the lead Forensic Crime Detective.

"We searched the area for hours and found a string and a marker," Detective Carlson said. He had been with the forensic crime squad going on ten years.

"That's about it. This is one clean crime scene. Maybe we'll get a break and there's some DNA or something."

"Thanks. I think our best hope might be the nightclub the victim was at last night. She left with this guy. I know it."

"Good luck," Carlson said, truly meaning it, knowing they didn't have much to go on right now.

Lance nodded and walked closer to where Jessica's body had been discovered. Earlier in the day, Reid intensely questioned the jogger that discovered the body and felt certain he wasn't involved.

He looked up and out into the crowd that had gathered. Onlookers, the curious, along with the news media.

Are you out there you bastard, looking, watching, smiling?

Lance scanned the crowd.

That sick feeling started to take over him. It all started when he was a teenager. What happened to his sister had nearly destroyed his family forever, and then Uncle Nate. Lance knew he had to push that feeling away. It was another reason why he was here and did what he did. Why he was a police officer, a homicide detective. Lance would never forget.

Lance looked over his shoulder. Some twenty feet away was Claire's photographer. He was watching everything the detectives were doing. Lance thought there was something odd about it, the way he was staring, like he was surveying the area. Then Lance watched Claire walk up to the guy and touch his arm.

Lance instantly felt angry and jealous. He turned away and started walking back to his truck. It was time to go back to the police department, get an update on the investigation on what his team had managed to come up with, and, get ready for his live news interview. He'd have to deal with his personal feelings about Claire another day.

After Officer Pierce finished with his late afternoon news conference in the parking lot down from where detectives still worked the murder scene, Channel Four grabbed Pierce for an interview, but Claire didn't care. She felt she would have the latest, and with her live shot with Lance at six, and her interviews with Jessica's friends for the ten newscast, she thought she had the situation covered.

Exclusive was the name of the game.

Claire walked up to her live truck crew where cables were strung out everywhere and a microphone was laying on the ground where Claire would be standing. Chandler was intensely watching what was going on at the murder scene behind the setup.

Claire walked up behind him and touched his shoulder to get his attention.

"Hey, Chandler, is everything ready?"

It took Chandler a few moments to realize she was talking to him. It was like he was in a trance.

"Yeah, I'm set. Did you hear that girl was going to begin an internship at our station this summer?"

"No, where did you hear that?" Claire asked.

"I'm not sure, I just did."

"I need to verify that. It's important information. Someone at the station must have interviewed her and knew her."

Claire called Hillary.

"Newsroom."

"Hillary, did you know Jessica Campbell was going to intern for us this summer?"

"Oh, Claire, yeah, I just heard that. I think our News Director, Tim Hansen, interviewed her."

"Well, I'll need to interview him and have him in my next story. Maybe we can do a live shot at ten with him and he can talk about her."

"I don't think that's going to work. He's a friend of the Campbell family. He already told me he would feel uncomfortable doing an interview. You can use the information, but he doesn't want to be a part of it."

Claire was furious. She walked in a circle around the cables and microphone. Chandler and Greg could tell something was up.

"When did you find out? Why am I the last to know?"

"Hey, I just found out. You already left with Greg to come here."

"And when was someone going to take the time to tell me?"

"Look, I'm only passing on the information. I was going to tell you before the news, but I had to verify with our News Director first since... Oh. Got to go, we're less than ten minutes away from the start of the news."

Claire slammed shut her cell phone. She was trembling. She would use the information at 5pm news, so she had to calm down and get ready.

Claire bent over and picked the microphone up off the ground. She pulled her earpiece out of her pocket and bent over to connect it to the audio wire. She stood up, launching into her introduction, practicing what she was going to say before she went on the air.

"Test one, two, three. Jim, a horrible discovery this morning. A young coed from Dallas found murdered here behind me in this Midtown Park. Jessica Campbell was a student at Southern Methodist University where she was going to be a senior. Her parents are prominent in the community. Her father, Brandon Campbell, is a local banker and involved in the oil and gas business. Her mother, Ann Campbell, is a former attorney who now is deeply involved in Dallas charity work. Jessica was supposed to begin an internship this summer at our television station, KABC. Here's the latest."

Chandler at the camera and Greg at the live shot board had their headsets on and had listened to what Claire said. They always commented to her how they felt. Thumbs up or down.

Chandler signaled thumbs up.

"Claire, two minutes. Sounds good," Greg said as he adjusted the volume on the board.

Chandler kept his eye looking through the camera.

Claire could hear the news opening jingle and then Becky Martinez and Jim Marrs gave their opening comments.

Chandler counted her down with his finger, five, four, three, two, one.

"Good evening, Jim. A horrible discovery this morning."

Lance was at his desk at the police station after leaving the crime scene when all of the media started setting up, and now he was watching Claire on his iPad. He wasn't surprised when she announced that Jessica was supposed to begin working at the station.

He turned down the volume and turned away, looking down at reports Reid brought in earlier.

It looked as though the detectives had been thorough, interviewing several people around the area.

The forensics team was waiting on the results from the string they found. Spencer's report was the most unsettling. Jessica had been raped before she was strangled.

The bruising and tears indicated it was not consensual. It was something no parent wanted to know.

Spencer's report concluded that from evidence taken at the scene that Jessica more than likely was killed somewhere else, around three in the morning, and her body was dumped in the park right before five in the morning.

The early morning jogger may have stumbled across her just minutes after the killer had left her with a smiley face sticker on her neck, with only her torn blouse on. Spencer's report said there was no DNA left on the body and whoever put the sticker on Jessica didn't leave a trace of who he was. He was still checking out the puncture wound on her thigh and suspected it may have been a dart that had a substance that drugged her.

Tonight would be important, interviewing all the club patrons they could and the bartenders.

He was thirty minutes away from doing his live interview with Claire.

Reid came in, followed by Crawford, Davis and Spencer.

"Do you know what happened to Jessica?" Lance asked his detective team. "She was raped, murdered by strangulation and then dumped at the park."

Lance waved the reports in the air with his hand.

"This doesn't cut it. Tonight we are going to the Dixie Club and interviewing patrons and bartenders. Jessica left with her killer and someone saw it. I want the last fifty-two hours of Jessica's life in a report tomorrow."

With that last comment Lance looked down. He was angry and frustrated.

The detectives slowly filed out of his office, including Reid.

Lance stood and walked to the window, looking down at the mass media collecting now outside of the Dallas Police station. Lance had no idea what he was going to say tonight.

He wondered if Claire's usual photographer would be with her at the live shot. Lance didn't know why, but there was something about that photographer he did not like.

I need to have him checked out, he thought. Hell, I need to have everyone checked out, even my own.

With the live shot finished for the five newscast, the television crew started breaking down to move to the next location at the downtown Dallas Police department.

Chandler began to dismantle his camera and put it in his car.

Claire finished her cell phone conversation and turned to Chandler.

"We have an interview with three of Jessica's friends, two of them were at the Dixie Club with her last night. We need to be there in ten minutes."

"We need to shoot a news tease tonight about the exclusive interviews," Claire said. "Can you make sure it gets edited?"

"Sure, stand there and let's use the crime scene and police in the background." She turned back toward the camera.

"Good evening, I'm Claire McKenzie, Dallas police continue to investigate the murder of Jessica Campbell, now being called The Smiley Face Killer, after it was revealed the suspect left a smiley face sticker on her neck. Join me tonight at ten for an exclusive interview with Jessica's friends from college, devastated over the loss of their best friend. Tonight on Channel Two News at ten."

"Let's record the tease for the six newscast," Greg said.

"Ok. Good evening. I'm Claire McKenzie. Tonight on Channel Two News at six, we'll have the latest on the Smiley Face murder as I interview lead Dallas Homicide Detective Lance Harris. Join us at six."

"How's that?"

"Fine."

Standing in the newsroom, purse, keys and cell in hand, Melissa dialed on her cell phone. It was ringing. Claire answered.

"Can you get there in ten?" Melissa asked.

"Yeah, we'll leave now," Claire said as she started moving towards Chandler.

"I'm not going. You'll have to take Greg. I need to get back and re-edit some video and shots I think need to go in your story for the six newscast."

"Chandler, it's fine the way it is—this is big and another exclusive for us," Claire said, clearly exasperated by Chandler's attitude.

"I told you I'm going back to the station. Greg can handle it."

"What's wrong with you, Mister 'I want to scoop

64

everyone'? I want to get this killer. This is the kind of interview you thrive on. What's going on?"

"Claire, nothing is going on. I'm out of here." And Chandler grabbed his camera and headed to his Viper parked about eight feet away.

He placed his equipment in the backseat, jumped in the front, started the engine and sped away.

Claire stood, shocked about what had transpired between her and Chandler. She was having a bad day today when it came to men.

Claire was trying not to cry. Then she turned and ran to the live truck where she caught Greg putting the audio board in the back of the news van.

"Hey, girl, what's up?"

"I'm not sure. I have an exclusive interview set up in between newscasts and Chandler said he can't do it because he has to re-edit my story with some video for the six newscast. Greg, can you help me and shoot the interviews?"

"Sure thing. Sounds strange to me, too. Hop in. We need to hurry if we're going to make it on time."

"We need to go to the Starbucks on Mockingbird Lane down from that new nightclub the Dixie Club."

Off Greg drove in the news van.

Claire was quiet on the ride there, trying to figure out what in the world was going on. What was with Chandler? Something is going on. Claire closed her eyes, exhausted, and she still had five more hours to go before she could even think about going home.

Claire knew she would only have twenty minutes to do the interviews and that she would be arriving at her live shot with five minutes to spare.

Maybe she should call Lance and let him know she was running late. No, he might ask her what was going on, and she didn't want Lance to know about the interviews, or her plans to go to the club tonight.

Forget it! Lance and Chandler can deal with each other.

Claire heard Greg talking on his cell phone to the station. Greg was in charge of the Engineering Department and planned the live shot lineup every night for all three newscasts.

"You're going to need to send Raphael to set up for the live shot at the downtown police station. We are going to swing by and do some interviews and we're going to barely make it."

Claire could hear someone arguing in the background.

"Look, I don't give a shit about a new baby elephant at the zoo. You tell Raphael to tear down now and get his butt over there. Tell him to make sure the microphone is on and ready to go."

Greg flipped his cell phone shut.

"I hope we can make it."

"We will," Claire said as she pointed her finger straight ahead. "There's the Starbucks right there."

"Maybe we will make it." And Greg gave the van a hard right turn into the parking lot.

Melissa was inside of the coffee shop with the three young ladies, all in their early twenties, getting ready to graduate soon and start their new lives. Claire remembered how excited she was when she was offered and accepted the job at Channel Two.

Melissa had already started taking notes like it was her story. She should be the one doing this, not Claire. She was the one who made all of the calls. Melissa was ambitious, and she knew this story could be the way to the television airwaves. She knew she wanted to be a news reporter before she left for college, and she knew if she worked hard at this internship they would welcome her back with open arms. Melissa wasn't going to let anyone stand in her way. Claire could see it in her body expression and her eyes when she turned towards Claire.

Jessica's three friends sat at a table for six in the coffee shop. You could tell they had all been crying with swollen, bloodshot eyes.

Melissa had grabbed a Frappuccino for everyone, but no one had taken a sip.

Melissa, who was a brunette, thought it was strange that they all looked alike, like Jessica. They all had long blonde hair, perfect bodies, green, brown or blue eyes and they were all carrying the perfect purse, a Coach or Louis Vuitton.

Melissa turned her head towards the door when she heard all the commotion.

It was Claire. People recognized her, started asking her questions. She was talking to the manager, making sure she had clearance to tape the interviews here, something Melissa knew she should have thought of and taken care of.

Claire strolled towards the tables. There was silence in the coffee shop.

Claire greeted Melissa first, which surprised her.

"Melissa, you are outstanding. Thank you."

Turning toward the three women.

"Girls, I want to tell you how sorry I was to hear about Jessica. I learned late this afternoon that she was going to start an internship at our station."

Sticking her hand out for a proper introduction, "Claire McKenzie, and I want you to know we will do everything we can to find out who did this."

There was Katherine Mays, a junior at Southern Methodist University, studying to become a doctor. Suzanne Hawkins, a student at the University of Texas with a major in geology. And Deidra Womack who attended Texas Christian University in Fort Worth in the Fine Arts Department, hoping someday to become a famous ballerina or take a chance in the film industry. They all grew up with Jessica, since junior high. They all came from Dallas families.

"Suzanne already talked to one police officer," Deidra said. As the conversation continued, Greg silently set up the cables, camera and microphone to get ready for the interview. Claire and Greg decided earlier that they would not only tape the interview but feed it back live to the television station to make sure nothing went wrong. A backup plan. As Claire started the interview, Greg was rolling. It was being taped and recorded live back at the television station.

"Ladies, I'm sorry. I only have fifteen minutes, so I want to start with you telling me about Jessica."

There was a small gathering of spectators, customers already in the Starbucks, gathering and watching with curiosity what was happening. The manager was doing his best to keep them at a distance.

"She was beautiful, smart and knew what she wanted to do, and that's become a journalist like you," Suzanne said. "She would never do anything stupid. The police are wrong on that. Jessica would never leave with just anyone. It wasn't like her."

"I understand all of you were at the Dixie Club last night," Claire asked.

"Suzanne and I were," Katherine said. "Deidra came later. Jessica kept disappearing, but there were so many of our friends there last night, most of them back in town from college for the summer, that I didn't think anything about it. Then Jessica came up and said she was leaving. She told me it was someone she knew who could help her with her career. She ran off so fast I didn't get a chance to ask her his name." Katherine started sobbing. "It's my entire fault. I didn't ask her who she was leaving with. I should have been more of a friend, but instead, some stupid song came on and I went out on the dance floor." She cradled her face in her hands, sobbing uncontrollably, and Suzanne and Deidra put their arms around her.

"Claire, five minutes and then we have to leave," Greg told her.

"Suzanne, did Jessica have a boyfriend?"

"It was on and off with Brad, but we never saw anything violent. We never, ever, thought anything like that."

"It's not him," Deidra softly spoke up. "I was walking in with three other people. I saw Jessica and waved at her. She waved back. I noticed she was leaving with a tall guy with dark hair and broad shoulders, like he played sports or worked out, but I only saw him from the back. Brad showed up a few minutes later and closed the place down with the rest of us. I didn't think anything about it. Brad said he talked to Jessica earlier and was expecting to meet her at the club when he got off work. I think he was a little disappointed because Jessica left without telling him. I know he tried her cell and never got an answer. There were so many of us from school that I think he was caught up in the reunion atmosphere at the club like we were."

"I'm with Suzanne, Jessica would never have left with anyone she didn't know. She was not that type, ever."

"Was anything bothering her? Was she upset about anything?" Claire questioned.

Clearly trying to hold it together, allowing tears to run down her face, Deidra answered. "She called me the day before she left. She was so happy about her life, school and excited about her career. There's no way she was depressed. Whoever she went with she knew."

"Claire, it's time."

"I'm sorry to leave. I appreciate it that you came down to meet with me for the interview. I hope we catch this killer and fast. Here is my business card. I put my cell number on the back. Please call me if you remember anything or if something comes up."

Claire rose from the table.

"We like your reporting, and we know you won't sensationalize this."

Katherine gained her composure. "Not like some of those other reporters who are hell-bent on making Jessica look like some slut."

Claire started to leave for the door, "Thank you for those kind words. I'll be in touch. Melissa, I'll see you back at the station after my live shot. We need to take off."

"Yes, I understand."

Greg had already packed up the equipment. Claire ran for the door and jumped in the van as Greg sped away for the Dallas Police Department. He was on the cell phone with someone. Claire wasn't sure who, but she thought it might be Chandler.

"He's there, set up and waiting for Detective Harris to come down. It's thirteen minutes until the beginning of the news. Go ahead and think about what you want to say in the open and I'll get us there, hopefully, with a few minutes to spare." And with that, Greg hit the gas and plunged the van into high gear, definitely over the speed limit.

Claire was trying to get her thoughts together. She had taken some notes, but she decided to jot down some questions. What is the latest in the investigation? Do you have a suspect? How did Jessica die? Have you talked to her parents? The rest would come during the interview.

Greg slammed to a quick halt in front of the police department and Claire exited the car and started walking towards the side of the building where Chandler was set up. She could see Raphael pulling a last minute cable.

Claire saw Lance and her heart skipped a beat. He was on his cell phone but standing with two other female detectives. Claire thought he was so handsome.

"I need to get a grip," Claire said to herself.

Claire briskly walked across the steps to the grassy area.

She noticed Chandler was staring at Lance and then he saw her and motioned for her to grab the microphone.

"You're late."

"Don't worry; I have our interviews for the ten newscast. What are you doing here anyway?"

Chandler never answered her. He stepped back as Greg walked up with the camera and set it up for Claire, checking in with the station for time and countdown until they went live.

Claire was sick of all men. Then she felt a hand on her back, a familiar hand, one she wanted to stay on her body forever.

"I see you're running crazy like I am," Lance softly whispered in her ear.

Claire smiled up at him.

"I am. Tell me you have him."

"No, we don't."

"One minute."

"You ready?"

"As ready as I'll ever be."

Claire adjusted her earpiece and heard the anchor read the intro before the camera turned to her.

Claire said a few words before pitching her story. After the story aired the camera was back live on her and Lance.

At first Claire asked the usual questions concerning the investigation and status of a suspect, then she changed the tone of her questioning.

"Detective Harris, I have interviewed three of Jessica's close friends and they say she rarely dated and would never leave with someone she didn't know. What angle has the investigation taken?"

"There's no angle," Harris said between clinched teeth. "We are looking at everything and everyone. We will find the person who did this, I promise you," Harris said looking straight into the camera.

"Thank you for your time, Detective." Claire turned to wrap up her segment and Greg eased the camera in for a close-up shot while Claire finished.

"Tonight at ten we will have exclusive reaction from three of Jessica Campbell's close friends, devastated over what has happened to Jessica. Claire McKenzie, Channel Two News."

Chandler signaled a wrap.

Claire put down the microphone.

Lance grabbed her arm.

"We need to talk," he said, practically dragging Claire around the side of the building. "What was that all about?"

"Some of her friends think you and your detectives have their minds made up that she was some kind of floozy and just left with a guy."

"Off the record. I don't believe that for a minute. So your information is way off."

Lance pulled his fingers through his dark brown hair, clearly frustrated with the investigation, with Claire, with everything.

"Listen, I can't meet you tonight. I have to work."

Claire had to work as well, but she thought they could meet after she finished the late news. For all of his signals this morning, Lance had changed his mind and it hurt...again.

"Don't worry about it. I have something I have to take care of anyway and I'm working late. Who do I talk to for the latest information for my story?"

"Does this something have to do with someone else?"

"Yes, it does. Now who do I talk to so I can get the latest information for my story, Officer Pierce?"

Claire was mad and her ego was bruised. She couldn't believe she let herself fall into that trap, believing this morning that he wanted to see her, maybe even date her again.

"Contact Officer Pierce." Lance walked away from her and

started climbing the steps to the front door of the police department.

Claire watched as Lance walked away. She was not sure why she let Lance think there was someone else, except she wanted to hurt him.

Because of his rejection tonight, she knew it was another dumb move.

Lance slammed open the door and headed to his office, madder than hell. He should have known there was someone else. He should have shown more interest in her and not have blamed it on work. Once again, too late.

CHAPTER EIGHT

Lance welcomed the cool air inside after being out in the heat doing the live interview with Claire. It helped clear his head and his mind since it was more than the outside heat he was feeling, being around Claire. At least the pounding in his head finally stopped. Lance waved at the front desk commander and started making his way through the throng of people who were in the hallway waiting for the elevators.

As he punched in the elevator button he looked over and saw the police chief's wife, Tiffany. She was talking to two other police officers, and when the elevator doors opened Lance practically leaped inside, turned and prayed for the metal doors to close, hoping Tiffany didn't see him. Thankful no one else had stepped inside the elevator, Lance wasn't in the mood to talk. He had to think. One more quick meeting and then on to the club.

The doors opened and Lance descended down the hall towards his office. He passed the open area where several of his detectives were. Reid was on the phone and looked intent about who he was talking with.

Lance spied Davis as he looked up from his desk and pile of papers.

He signaled for Davis to join him in his office. Shaun looked up, nodded his head and pointed to the phone, letting

Lance know he needed to finish his phone call. Lance walked inside his office and sat at his desk, covered with paper and files from the investigation.

Reid walked into Lance's office carrying a cup of coffee and his notebook. He sat down in a chair in the back of the room. Two other detectives along with Davis, Reid, and Ryan were working the case around the clock. Everyone looked tired and angry, Lance thought.

"Let's get started. Shaun will be here in a minute," Lance said.

"Reid, bring everyone up to date on what we were able to find out last night."

"Lance and I are going to the Dixie Club tonight to interview people who saw Jessica. She definitely left with a man last night. She knew him, according to statements made by her girlfriends. Let's chart her activities the last forty-eight hours."

Reid stood and walked over to the board someone wheeled in earlier. He took a marker and wrote down *Tuesday*, the date and nine am.

"Here's what we know so far. Tuesday morning, Jessica has coffee and breakfast with her mother around nine in the morning. Her mother, Ann, said Jessica took a shower and then left with Katherine Mays around eleven that morning. Katherine and Jessica went shopping at the mall, and she told us Jessica was excited because she had found out she would be doing an internship at Channel Two."

"Do we know who she interviewed with?" asked Davis.

"She interviewed with the Channel Two News Director, Tim Hansen. He said he hired her to work this summer. He said he left her a message on her cell phone late yesterday afternoon, so we can assume that she heard the message that she had been hired. What confuses me is why Jessica didn't immediately tell her parents. Her cell phone remains missing, so we don't know if she received the news."

"Not anymore," Shaun said excitedly as he walked into Lance's office. He waved a sheet of paper in the air. "Here's the information. A teenager came in to Cutter's Pawn Shop and tried to pawn a new black Samsung cell phone. The owner just called in to let us know. I need to run over there fast. They have the teenager tied up in a chair so he won't get away until I interview him."

"Take Ryan with you. He's out there in the office. I want the rest of the team to hear what we have."

"Sure, Captain, I'll call you after I find out what's going on and get a good look at that phone," Shaun said as he sprang up to leave the office. Lance called out to him.

"Make sure our computer geeks get it pronto."

Then Lance watched as Shaun called over to Ryan Elliot.

"Okay, let's get back to it."

"Has the News Director been cleared?" Davis asked as he walked in on the end of the conversation, taking a seat in a chair next to Lance's desk.

"Yes, he has an alibi," Lance replied.

Reid continued, glancing at the information in his notebook.

"Jessica returned home from shopping around four in the afternoon. Katherine said they saw some girlfriends out shopping. She said a man, apparently a stranger, asked Jessica a question about a piece of jewelry when the two were looking at earrings, and that he 'appeared creepy,' were her exact words, so she and Jessica left the jewelry section without buying anything. Katherine said she didn't notice anyone suspicious or didn't notice if anyone was following them. They did purchase several clothing items and shoes, but no jewelry."

"Should we go to the mall and interview the clerks, or even find out what time they were in the jewelry department, and stake it out to see if our stranger danger returns? He might be scoping women out," Davis said, turning towards Lance.

"That's a good idea. Do that. Tag it for later, though. I think we have more pressing things to do right now."

Davis shook his head, acknowledging Lance's request.

"Reid, what's next?"

"Ann said her daughter went upstairs to her bedroom. She thinks Jessica laid down for a nap. Jessica came down to the kitchen around six. She ate an apple that was in a big fruit bowl sitting on the kitchen counter. Jessica told her mother she was going out to dinner with her boyfriend, Brad, later that evening. She left to get ready. Katherine came to the house and picked Jessica up around seven. We know she went to the Dixie Club and never met up with her boyfriend, who repeatedly tried to call her."

"Davis, what do we have on the boyfriend?" Lance asked.

"Jessica and Brad have been dating about a year. He is twenty-five years old and attends Southern Methodist University. Makes decent grades. He has one more year, maybe a year and a half more, before he graduates with an engineering degree. No criminal record except for an arrest for criminal mischief when he was fourteen. He and some buddies were caught past curfew, and some of the boys had been throwing rocks at streetlights. They all received a sentence to serve community service. He appears to be devastated about what happened to Jessica. He said he would take a lie detector test, but his parents have hired an attorney and slammed the door on that happening." Davis paused. "I just don't think he's our guy. Jessica's friends say he was with them until closing at the Dixie Club. I'm just going with my gut on this. This is someone who has done this before and will do it again until he is caught."

"I want to talk to the boyfriend again," Lance told Davis. "Davis, set it up for me. Maybe she said something about working at the TV station or mentioned people she met there."

"Sure thing, Captain."

Reid wrote down 11pm on the chalkboard.

"The night before she was murdered, Jessica and boyfriend returned home at eleven at night. They went into the media room and watched a movie until two in the morning and then Brad left. Jessica reportedly went to bed. Ann did say she thought she heard Jessica moving around, but she said she fell back asleep. There was nothing unusual that morning. Ann said Jessica appeared happy and looking forward to being with her friends."

Lance picked up a piece of paper that was on his desk and began reading the information out loud to the detectives.

"This is preliminary, but here's what Spencer Wyatt thinks," Lance said. Looking down again he continued.

"Jessica was killed sometime between three and five in the morning. There were signs that she had been sexually active, but at this point we don't know if it was consensual or if she was assaulted. Spencer thinks she was raped, and we are waiting on the results of the injection in her thigh. There was no sperm found on her, so we can assume the perp used a rubber or didn't ejaculate. We'll know more when the test results come back. She died from strangulation, but get this, Wyatt thinks the suspect strangled her from behind because of the imprints of his fingers found around her neck. So it looks as though she didn't know it was coming and that's why there are signs of trauma on her legs. She must have tried to kick him. Comments?"

"So this is different from the Smiley Face murders of the past?" Davis asked.

"Even though the smiley face sticker was stuck on her neck like the other victims, Jessica didn't know what was coming. Can we consider then that she was murdered somewhere else and her body was dumped at the park since the area around her was clean?"

"I'm convinced of that," Reid said. "He either panicked and dumped her body or he had it planned like this all along."

"Okay. Listen up. Here's the plan now. Let's go through the media and find out if anyone else was in the park and if they saw anything. I'll follow up with Wyatt on the autopsy reports and get back to you. Reid, finish your report on Jessica's comings and goings and pass that out. Then I want everyone interviewed who came in contact with her, let's say, the last four days. That includes her interview at the television station. I want to know everyone she talked with and met there at the station."

Lance paused.

"I want the sack boy at the grocery store interviewed. I want to talk to everyone who came in contact with her the last four days, and that includes her parents. Have that report back to me ASAP. I'm going to be out on an assignment tomorrow, so report everything to Reid until I return. We'll let you know if we learn anything after we do our interviews at the Dixie Club tonight. You're dismissed."

Lance stood as everyone filed out of his office and back to work.

"You ready?" He reached behind his chair to retrieve his sports jacket, slipping his arms through the sleeves.

"Let's head to the Dixie Club. I'm sure it's starting to get busy."

Lance and Reid walked down the hall in silence.

The blast of humidity hit them as they opened the back door and headed for Lance's truck. Lance took his keys, put them in the starter and the engine roared alive.

"I'm going to Huntsville tomorrow to see Watkins, but I don't want anyone to know about it. I think he's our key."

"Have fun listening to him scream about his innocence," Reid replied.

"My gut tells me he knows something."

Greg and Claire were leaving the police station and were on their way to the station to edit her story for the ten newscast when they saw Lance and Sanchez pass by.

"Let's follow them and see where they are going."

Greg pulled a U-turn.

Claire spied Lance parking his truck in the lot of the Dixie Club.

"Hey, Greg, guess where we're going after I finish my story?"

"The Dixie Club. We might even do a live shot from there. Something to think about."

"Right on."

In the car on the way to the club, Lance casually asked Reid if Claire was seeing anyone.

"I saw her with a guy, Eric Thomas, I think a couple of times, but there didn't seem to be much there," Reid said. "I think that's the name she introduced."

"Check him out. I want to know everything," Lance said.

"Okay." Reid glanced across at Lance, wondering what was going on.

Moments later they pulled into the parking lot at the Dixie Club.

Lance parked close to the front door, sliding the police sign on his dash in case they needed to leave quickly. With badge in hand, a gun inside their jackets and their cell phones, they walked to the door at the club. A bouncer was standing in the doorway as they entered.

Lance flashed his badge. "Detective Harris and Detective Sanchez. We are here to see the manager and interview your bartenders, waitresses and people who were here last night."

"One moment Detective," the tall black guy said as he walked towards the back of the club.

Three ladies came rolling in, laughing and looking ready

for a night on the town. They smiled at Harris and Sanchez as they walked by.

"Hey, handsome, want to have some fun? Look for me!" one yelled as the others continued laughing and shrieking as they walked in the club.

Lance and Reid looked at each other.

"Oh, well," Lance said.

The black guy by the name of Hunter returned. "Gentlemen, please follow me."

Lance and Sanchez entered what felt like a dark cave with music, dancing and drinking, the signature of the club. The waitresses were dressed in costumes to make them look like Pebbles on the old *Flintstones* television show.

The music was so loud you couldn't talk to the person next to you. They entered a room slightly hidden beside one of the bars, where crowds of people waited for a drink.

A tall, thin, older, blond-haired man approached them as they stood barely inside the nightclub.

"John McCartney, owner and manager of the Dixie Club. I understand you want to do some interviews."

"Detective Harris, Detective Sanchez. We specifically would like to talk to the bartender who may have served Jessica Campbell. A waitress, anyone who may have seen her."

"This way. I was expecting you."

The three men walked into the black cave, dodging dancing women, men standing in groups and young people standing or sitting at various tables throughout the club.

The DJ played a song, "Tattoos On This Town," by country singer Jason Aldean. The women were swaying and singing along to the popular song.

McCartney stopped in front of a tall, blonde girl who had just served drinks.

"Julie, can you come with me for a few moments?"

Julie nodded and followed the three men back behind the

bar into a room that resembled a party room. All it needed were the decorations, food and booze.

McCartney offered a table and chairs as everyone sat down.

"Julie, I am Detective Harris and this is Detective Sanchez. I understand you saw Jessica Campbell and served her a couple of drinks last night?"

"Yes sir, we had a meeting in here with Mr. McCartney so that we could all talk about who saw her and what all we saw to refresh our memory."

Lance looked over at McCartney but did not smile. McCartney shrugged. More like covering your ass, Lance thought. He had specifically told McCartney to let him talk to everyone first.

"Did you see Jessica?"

"Yes sir, I was serving her table. There were several girls and a couple of guys. They had pushed four tables together, close to the dance floor. They seemed like a nice crowd. I remember Jessica because I overheard her telling her friends about her interview at Channel Two and how she was going to start interning this summer. It made me kind of jealous because I want to work in television news, but it's going to take me a while to get through community college since my parents are without jobs and I am having to work and put myself through school."

"It's great what you are doing, and I know you are going to do great in your career. What else do you remember about that night?" Sanchez urged Julie to continue.

"Well, there were lots of girls and guys in and out of the group. I remember one guy, tall with black hair. He looked familiar to me, like I had seen him before, but I got the feeling he wasn't part of their old high school crowd. I remember Jessica seemed kind of in awe of him. The next thing I knew, maybe twenty minutes later, I brought another round of drinks to the table and I noticed she was gone, along with that guy she was so intensely talking to. Her friends didn't seem too concerned, and one of them took care of her drinks and tip."

"Jessica didn't seem uneasy around him or nervous?" Lance asked.

"No, sir, she actually seemed kind of excited."

"If you saw him again do you think you could recognize him?"

"I think so."

"We're going to be out walking around here in a minute. If you see anyone who was around last night, if you could discreetly let us know. I would appreciate it."

Harris and Sanchez stood to say goodbye to Julie.

As she walked away, McCartney stood up as well.

"She's one of my best employees. I hope she makes it out of here. I'll be right back with the bartender who said he may have seen Jessica leave last night."

Lance remained standing, alone in his own thoughts.

The door swung open and in walked a heavyset guy, dark brown hair, looking to be in his early thirties.

"Frank Melon."

"Frank's been with us for about five years and is fairly familiar with the regulars," McCartney said.

"I'm Detective Harris and this is Detective Sanchez. Please sit down. What can you tell us about last night? Did you know Jessica Campbell and did you see her?"

"I've seen her around a couple of times. She never came directly up to the bar, but I was keeping an eye on that group when I could. Lots of good ass, if you know what I mean." Melon winked at them.

Neither Lance nor his partner showed any reaction.

"Anyway, I saw Jessica leaving with a guy. She was waving goodbye to everyone. I could only see him from behind, but he looked like someone I've seen before. Tall, big, dark hair, looked like he lifted weights. I never saw his face, only his back. Now that I think about it, he was making sure no one had a clear look at him. Then I was serving another round when I heard a guy in that group scream something: 'What the hell are you telling me that she left with someone,' and he sounded pissed. They were all trying to calm him down."

"When you say that you recognized him, how is that?"

"I can't explain it. Maybe he just looks like a lot of guys in there all the time. I never saw him, that guy that night, talking or being around anyone but that Jessica chick."

Frank sat there for a moment. No one said anything.

"This may sound weird, but it's like he was careful not to get noticed. I had a gut feeling he knew what he was doing. Too confident."

"Anything else you remember from that night?"

"Just the arrogance. He was an asshole, sorry."

"Thank you for your time. Please let us know if you remember anything," Lance said as he stood and handed him one of his cards.

"Yeah, okay," and he left.

All three men stood again.

"Mr. McCartney."

"Please call me John." He shook hands with Lance.

"Here is our information if anything else comes up. Do you have any surveillance camera video we can look at from last night?"

"Of course. Let me get with Joseph and he'll get it for you."

"Thanks. Do you mind if we walk around and see if we hear or see anything for a while?"

"No, just be as discreet as you can."

"Thank you again for your cooperation," Sanchez said as the three men walked out of the party room and back behind the bar to come out into the nightclub again.

Lance didn't see Claire standing across the room from him as he started walking, listening to the club talk.

Claire and Greg arrived at the Dixie Club. Things were hopping, even though everyone knew a girl was murdered last night after she left the club.

People wanting to be in on the action or be a part of the latest. Claire hung back in the shadows, watching Lance at work.

Chandler offered to edit her story after she laid her voice down on the voice track so she and Greg could take off.

The television station had been promoting the exclusive interviews with Jessica's friends throughout prime time, so she knew they would have a big audience tonight.

Claire was waiting to hear from Chandler if he wanted to do the live shot from the murder scene or if she needed to be on the anchor desk for the ten newscast. At least Greg was with her in case she went live from the club.

CHAPTER NINE

It was dark now. Just the way he liked it. He looked out at where he had dumped her body at the park. The news media was beginning to arrive again to do a live shot for the ten newscast.

It was just the way he likes it. Everything in turmoil and no one knew a damn thing—especially those idiot cops. He smiled at the thought that the news media had tagged him the "Smiley Face Killer." Time to get back to work. How sweet it is.

It was after nine when Claire's cell phone rang. She'd been discreetly following Lance around the nightclub, making notes on everyone he interviewed. Greg left earlier to get something to eat and was waiting for her phone call to tell him where the live shot was going to be.

"Hello, this is Claire McKenzie."

"Meet me at the murder scene by 9:45," Chandler said and then hung up.

"Goodness. What is his problem?" Claire whispered.

The loud music in the club was starting to give her a headache. She needed to call Greg and let him know she was ready to be picked up and that they needed to leave for the murder scene. He had gone outside earlier to get something to eat and to call his wife. The Dixie Club wouldn't allow cameras inside, so Greg could only tape outside shots for her story.

"Chandler had better finish my story and it better be good," she whispered as she turned to leave and collided right into Lance.

"If it's not Ms. McKenzie," Lance snarled as he softly grabbed both of her arms, not allowing her any way to escape. "And what business would you have here at the Dixie Club? Don't you need to be getting ready for your late newscast and your exclusive story? I have known you were here the whole time."

"Let me go. I was just leaving," Claire said as she squirmed to get free from Lance's grip. Mad at herself for being caught.

He leaned in to her. At first she thought crazily that he might kiss her.

Lance quietly whispered in her ear, "Claire, I want you to be careful. I mean it. This is serious," as he released her arms and walked back to Reid, who had stopped what he was doing and was watching their confrontation.

Claire spun on her heels and marched right through the middle of the club to the front door.

"Hey, aren't you that news reporter Claire McKenzie?" a drunk, twenty-something guy yelled out. "Come home with me tonight, sweet thing."

The last thing Claire saw as she was exiting the front door was Lance and Reid confronting the guy and making him sit down.

When she'd made it outside Claire punched Greg's number into her cell phone.

"What's up?"

"Chandler said to meet him at the park for the ten live shot."

"I am around the corner. Be there in a few," Greg said.

She flipped shut her cell and tried her best to blend into the outside crowd.

Waiting, Claire thought about how Greg had left to see his wife. Now there was a man with his priorities right. Greg was a good, honest man. They had been married a long time. Claire prayed someday to have that relationship.

"Yep, a keeper," Greg would laugh and say about his wife, Claire thought to herself, smiling. Greg arrived and they were on their way.

Claire and Greg arrived at Memorial Park, the scene of the crime, and as always, Chandler had set up the camera in the best position and background, leaving the other television stations scrambling to find a spot.

Greg parked the truck next to the television station's live truck.

"Why does Chandler have to be so off the wall all the time?" Claire stressed as she climbed out of the truck. "Why does he have to be an asshole?" she said as she slammed the door, not giving Greg the opportunity to tell her to be careful.

"There's something wrong with that guy," Greg muttered.

Claire walked up to where Chandler was standing by his camera.

"Claire, where have you been? It's 9:50. Don't you think you are cutting it close?" Chandler said in a mocking tone.

"You know what, Chandler? Screw you, and leave me the hell alone," Claire yelled. "It's been a hell of a day, and I don't need your bullshit." Claire turned and flipped open her cell phone and called the station.

"Melissa, it's Claire. What do I need to say for an intro to my story, and how does it look?" Claire searched for her earpiece in her purse.

"I'd go with the latest, how the detectives were at the Dixie Club interviewing patrons, looking for someone who may have seen something suspicious. You can go through what all happened and then say something like, 'Here are some comments from friends of Jessica's we met with today at a local Starbucks,'" Melissa said.

Someone was yelling at Melissa in the background, Claire realized. "No, she's there and ready," she said. "Claire, wing it and good luck. One other thing: Chandler was editing your story to include the interviews, and then he dumped it on me, saying he had another assignment. He looked angry as usual."

"Melissa, don't worry about it, and thanks for backing me up. Got to check my makeup. I'll see you tomorrow."

But Melissa disappeared after leaving the television station later that night, sending the City of Dallas into a tailspin wondering if there was another serial killer.

CHAPTER TEN

Claire was shaking her head, wondering if what Melissa just told her confirmed something was up with Chandler. It wasn't like him to dump everything and leave early. But then again, he had been acting crazy since their interaction at the station.

Claire found her earpiece and pulled out her compact to check her lipstick as she walked to the camera. Chandler handed her the clip-on mike but didn't say anything to her. She shifted a few steps to get in position for the ten newscast.

Claire heard the news open and the anchors talking about the horrific murder of Jessica Campbell, the daughter of well-known Dallasites Brandon and Ann Campbell.

"On the scene tonight with the latest is Channel Two news reporter, Claire McKenzie. Claire, what can you tell us tonight?"

"Dwight, family and friends are mourning the loss of a beautiful young woman, Jessica Campbell, who was planning to come to work at our television station as an intern this summer. Tonight, investigators were at the Dixie Club interviewing clubgoers, bartenders and waitresses, trying to find out if anyone saw anything unusual or may have seen the man who left with Jessica. Tonight, News Two has an exclusive interview with three of Jessica's friends who say she would never leave with anyone she didn't know. Here's the latest."

The story rolled as Dallas watched Jessica's three friends share their grief.

"Dwight, tomorrow we'll find out more about what transpired from the interviews at the Dixie Club where Jessica was last seen leaving with a man described as having dark hair and a bodybuilder-type body."

"Claire, thanks for the latest. Hopefully the Dallas Police Department is onto this guy." Turning to another camera, "We'll have updates throughout the night on News Two."

Claire's face fell to her chest. Tears formed in her eyes. She was exhausted, but more than anything she was heartbroken about Jessica's death, especially after interviewing her friends. Claire was heartbroken for her family and friends. "She could've worked with me as a news reporter," Claire thought to herself.

Chandler and Greg started breaking down and hauling off the equipment to the news truck.

Claire just stood there, staring into space. She didn't move until Greg took her arm and led her to his truck. Chandler, she noticed finally, had already sped away in his flashy car.

"Greg, sometimes I just wonder how people can be so cruel. Jessica had everything going for her."

Greg hopped in the driver's seat and buckled his seat belt.

"Girl, I don't know what to tell you," Greg said as he turned his head to reverse out of the parking space.

"I'm worried about all of you. That's why I wanted to go home and see Dee before she had to go back downtown to work on her upcoming advertising presentation. Dee was mad when I left because she said I was acting like she was dumb or something, but this is the thing: I can't tell you why, but I get the feeling like this guy gets around. People know him. I told Dee that she and her friends need to stay in groups and don't talk to anyone. That goes for you, too, Claire. You and the girls at the station. I am really worried."

As Greg headed back to the station, Claire sat silently for a few moments.

"Greg, I'm scared, too. You're right. I believe Jessica's friends when they say she wouldn't have just left with anyone. She may not have known him all that well, but he made her feel comfortable enough to go with him. Now she's dead. Her family, friends, it is all devastating."

As Greg parked in the back of the station, he took hold of Claire's hand.

"I mean it, Claire, don't trust anyone. Not even people you know until the police get this guy."

Lance and Reid left the nightclub around 11:30 pm armed with new information. Two of the customers were coming into the station tomorrow to get a police sketch done.

As they were walking down the aisle, in between tables, they overheard a couple talking about the Campbell murder and if they thought the guy they saw last night could be the one responsible.

"Nothing wrong with taking a chance. It can only go one way. Either it's our big break or it's a bust."

No one spoke the rest of the drive back to the Dallas Police station.

Lance pulled in the parking lot, down from Reid's Chrysler. Sanchez got out. Before he closed the door he said, "Harris, we're missing something big time, and if we don't figure this out fast we're in a hell of mess and someone else is going to be dead."

Lance nodded in agreement but didn't have to say anything.

He knew.

Claire got home from the television station before midnight and unlocked the door. She went out back and fed her dogs. The automatic lights finally worked. She didn't like coming home to a dark house. In fact, she was getting tired of coming home to an empty house.

Her cell phone rang and she answered it. It was Eric. He could barely contain his anger. Claire tried to talk to him.

"Eric, remember we're meeting at Starbucks tomorrow. Goodnight." Claire hung up and closed her cell phone.

She was seeing a side of Eric she never realized before. She hated to admit it, but he was creepy. As she was hanging up on him, Eric told her the sexy things he was going to do to her tomorrow. She felt nauseated as she closed her cell phone.

Now Claire was scared, wondering what she had gotten herself mixed up in. Eric was tall with black hair and blue eyes. The first time Claire saw him at one of the local hangouts, he reminded her of the movie star Dermot Mulroney.

Claire was attracted to his crooked grin but now she saw a sinister side to it and she was frightened. Claire never realized how controlling Eric was until a big story broke a couple of weeks ago and he couldn't reach her and kept calling and calling.

As long as she was doing feature stories and home every night, things were fine. Even though they didn't have hardly any dates, thinking back now, it seemed Eric was fine just talking to her, knowing she was home alone. But there was always something about Eric that held Claire back. She always stopped everything. Claire wondered now if Eric would hurt her.

CHAPTER ELEVEN

The Smiley Face Killer was pacing the length of his studio condominium. He was excited about what happened last night, but angry about what transpired today, and all of the non-stop media coverage. He regretted what he'd been forced to do, but he didn't have a choice. He could have been recognized.

He stopped at his condo bar, grabbed a glass and some ice cubes from the small refrigerator and poured himself a scotch. With the first sip, calm settled over him and with the sweet burn going down his throat, he closed his eyes for a moment, remembering.

His parents had been wealthy. They lived in the University Park area. His father was an attorney. His mother a busy socialite. The younger brother was so into playing baseball, traveling with his select baseball team, he was never home to know what really was going on. Maybe he did know and he did it on purpose.

He remembered his parents were constantly screaming at each other behind closed doors in their bedroom. Apparently his father had a wandering eye. It's like they thought he was an idiot and never knew what was going on. Then they would walk out smiling, holding hands and head for the dining room for dinner. They would all sit down, every night, and act like nothing had happened or was going on.

Even though he made good grades and was a star athlete on the football team, he still managed to get in trouble. It was his temper. He started early, hurting small animals and then by the age of ten he would prowl the neighborhood late at night for larger animals. He had to stop when the local police started a surveillance task force because of the complaints of so many dead animals turning up. Having to stop nearly killed him, but it was then when he swore he would never get caught. His teammates were scared of him, even though they acted like his friends.

When he was in ninth grade he pushed one player down the stairs at the indoor facility, breaking his arm. No one said a word to school administrators, coaches, or teachers. Back then you didn't talk about things, but he had to lay low again.

When he turned seventeen, a classmate from his high school, Joanna Powers, who was sixteen at the time, disappeared. Police never found her body. He had to lay low again. He graduated and left for the University of Alabama where he had the time of his life.

Now, ten years later he was back where he wanted to be, in Dallas. He made a point of staying away from the places where old high school classmates might turn up. They were all busy having babies and doing all of that crap anyway. Another world that he would never care about. His parents had both died. His younger brother had taken off for California. They had not spoken in ten years. Didn't know where his other brother was. Wow, what a great family. Ha, at least that's the story he told.

No, as he finished sipping his drink, setting it on the bar, turning once again to look out at the Dallas skyline he was thinking, Man, I am having the time of my life and no one is ever going to know.

Claire barely slept at all during the night and finally gave up and crawled out of bed around six in the morning. Her bedroom was on the second floor. Sometimes she felt someone was watching her.

Someone was watching her with a telescope from beyond the shadows, catching a glimpse of her movements whenever he could.

Claire went into the kitchen to start coffee. As it brewed she tidied up in the kitchen. The beep signaled her coffee was ready. She poured herself a cup, headed for the refrigerator where she grabbed her favorite French vanilla creamer, poured it in her cup, took a sip and she knew her day was on its way. Claire turned to look out the kitchen window, outside at her patio. Still some things she wanted to do. Time for a party, Claire thought. But there were also other things to deal with.

When she arrived home last night and checked her messages, her parents had called and her brother. They were worried, but she couldn't deal with it all last night. She'd call them when she got to the office this morning.

Claire grew up in Dallas. Her father was a successful banker and her mother worked in advertising. She'd been a cheerleader in high school and was involved with ballet, taking ballet lessons since she was eight years old. Her younger brother, Michael, played football and was in college studying to be an engineer.

Claire knew she wanted to go to college and be a television journalist. Growing up she was fascinated with the latest news events.

Thinking back to 2009, President Barack Obama became the first African American United States President. 2010 the United States Economy was given another grim, gloomy forecast. In 2011 United States Special Forces killed Osama bin Laden, the suspected mastermind behind the September 11 terrorist attacks in America and the FBI's Most Wanted man, in Abbottabad, Pakistan, and the NASA Space Shuttle program ended with its final landing of the Space Shuttle Atlantis mission.

Claire's friends thought she was crazy because she was tuned to the television or her cell phone for the latest news events.

At college, Claire's journalism professor must've seen something in her because he was able to get her set up with the local ABC television affiliate, starting out as an intern, then working her way up to a reporter. Claire was live every night on the ten newscast, covering stories, crime and events she never dreamed existed. Claire was exhausted with work and finishing college, but she loved it.

Claire was tough, but it wasn't her way or the highway because she had a family scandal that changed her life and her family forever. That was another reason she wanted a career in journalism.

Claire never told any of her new friends at college what had happened. Claire's junior year in high school, her Uncle Henry was arrested for having sex with two minors, a sixteen-year-old girl and a seventeen-year-old girl. The two students had been a part of an internship called "Learn the Business," program over Christmas break. Uncle Henry was well known in the community, and he owned a successful electronics company.

Claire remembered just finishing cheerleader practice when her cell phone rang. It was her father. He told her what had happened and warned her to stay away from any news reporters who tried to talk to her. Claire was terrified trying to get to her car to go home.

Her uncle pleaded not guilty and his trial was set for four months later. The news media had been relentless because of who her uncle was, trying to dig up every negative thing or activity her uncle ever did.

The defense had wanted Claire to testify on her uncle's behalf because he had never acted inappropriately towards her. Claire was going to testify because her family told her she had to. The night before the trial was supposed to begin, Uncle Henry committed suicide. He left a note declaring his innocence. Claire's family was devastated. The news media went ballistic, and everyone was judge and jury, especially on social media.

Claire's family was never the same, and it took years for her father to get over what had happened to his brother, if he ever did.

No one ever knew what the truth was or what really happened. At family gatherings and on holidays, everyone tried to act like it was a happy time, but it wasn't.

Claire would never forget the time she and Michael were sitting out on the veranda at her grandmother Nina's house. Nina walked up the stairs and stopped in front of them.

"Michael, I want you to grow up to be the man God can be proud of and bless. Claire, I want you to grow up to be the woman God can be proud of and bless. You remember that on your journey through life," Nina said.

Nina never mentioned Henry's name, ever again, in front of them.

Claire knew then that in becoming a journalist, she would also be there for the victims of crime, and she wanted to help people. One year after graduating from college an older journalist that she had worked with, who had gone on to work at Channel Two, called to let her know there were two reporter openings in Dallas.

Claire called in every favor she could think of, and after three interviews she landed her dream job in Dallas.

Claire walked back to the kitchen, rinsed out her coffee cup and put it in the dishwasher.

Time to stop daydreaming and get ready for work. She

walked back up the stairs.

Claire was remembering how her grandmother had all of the sayings she would quote to the grandkids all the time, to keep them motivated.

Let's see, Claire thought, what was the one with the horse? Oh, yeah, Nina would tell her, "Pick yourself up off the ground and get back up in the saddle and ride again. Never give up!"

He was watching her now. He was down the street from Claire's house. He had rented the house as his second hideaway. He arrived around two in the morning. He watched as she moved through the house. On his bed were pictures of lovely girls. It made him hard just looking at them. But Claire was different and special.

He must remember that.

CHAPTER TWELVE

It was five in the morning as Lance checked his e-mail one last time and then walked through the kitchen out his back door to the garage.

He bolted the backdoor. He needed to get to Huntsville as soon as he could, and Watson had better be honest with him. Would anyone know he was gone? Lance got in his truck, opened the garage door and plugged his cell phone into the charger.

The necessities of life.

He planned to stop for coffee on his way out of Dallas. So far no word of another murder. He hoped Reid was able to cover for him and damn, it looked like the traffic was already backing up as Lance headed south on Interstate 45.

Reid was in the office by six in the morning. He quickly ran a check on Eric Thomas and waited for the results. He grabbed a cup of coffee and began the lineup sheet that Lance wanted all of the detectives to follow up on, specific leads.

As Reid sat down at his desk his phone rang.

"Sanchez."

"Hey Reid, I have the report on Thomas. What a sweet guy," Megan Conner said, the head of police records.

"What do you have?"

"Well, your Eric Thomas has been arrested twice for

sexual assault in San Antonio. Never convicted. He was questioned on another sexual assault while at college at SMU in Dallas, according to my sources, and all three times they had been girlfriends or ex-girlfriends. And get this, his friends stood by him every time."

"Great. Hey thanks, Megan. Can you send me a copy of everything you have?"

"On its way, Lieutenant."

Reid smiled as he hung up the phone. Megan was someone he could always count on, he thought. Maybe he should think about her in more terms than just as a great person who can get information fast. Yeah, maybe, as he grabbed his cell phone to call Lance. Claire was in danger. Could Thomas be the Smiley Face murderer? He would need to check him out more extensively.

Lance's voicemail came on. He must have already been inside the prison by now.

"Harris, call me ASAP. Claire may be in trouble."

Reid knew he was going to have to track Claire down himself if he didn't hear from Lance within the hour.

Back to reality, Claire walked back to the kitchen, rinsed out her coffee cup and put it in the dishwasher. She let her dogs in, closed and locked the door.

Time to get ready for work. She walked back up the stairs, to shower, dress, and get ready to face a new day.

Claire got to work early, wanting to stay ahead. Overnight it was quiet, thank goodness, she thought. For the early news they had recycled her story from the ten newscast.

Carrying her tote bag full of all of her necessities from makeup to her personal computer, she stopped by the coffee counter and grabbed another cup of coffee before she headed to her desk.

The morning show crew was in, already on live with the latest news. Thankfully, the story Claire re-edited last night after the late news was still current, or so she hoped.

Sitting down at her desk, turning on her computer, she went directly to her calendar for any stories she needed to follow up on. Nothing pressing, but she'd have to check on the status of the County Commissioner investigation sometime this week.

It was Thursday. The newsroom looked like a big circle of desks with computers everywhere, with the assignments editor and the lead producer in the middle, everyone lined up where they needed to be.

Claire made her calls and wondered why she couldn't get through to the Communications Department, so she decided to call Lance. He's not available either? She decided to track Chandler down and talk to him about a new angle to her story.

No answer. "Where is everyone?" Claire said aloud to no one but herself.

CHAPTER THIRTEEN

Traffic started to thin out as he left the Dallas city limits and drove down the highway towards Huntsville. Lance mulled over all they knew so far about the latest 'Smiley Face' murder. Then his thoughts turned to Claire.

"Why do I have to be an asshole?" he muttered. Lance didn't know what to do about Claire at this point. He was totally frustrated.

Shaking his head, out loud he said, "Boy, I sure acted mature last night. What an asshole."

Lance turned to what was ahead for him. He could see the state prison in the distance.

Huntsville was the oldest prison in Texas with its red brick walls and long winding street entrance. He parked as close to the front as he could. As he stepped out of his truck, he walked toward the check-in point. Lance could tell it was already in full swing inside the prison.

Everything should go fast and furious.

He'd been cleared for the meeting with Watson the day before, and since Lance called ahead on his cell phone to tell them an estimated time of arrival, the prison guards should be waiting in the hallway of the outside cells along the interview rooms ready to bring Watson to him.

At the first check in, Lance pulled out his badge to show

the prison officer.

"Lance Harris, Dallas Police," he said.

That claustrophobic feeling threatened Lance because of the feeling of being closed in. It happened every time he had to come to the prison.

The gated doors opened and Lance walked down the stark white hallway to his next stop, one of three, before he was led into the cage-like visitation rooms.

Lance walked up to the check-in counter.

"Sir, your ID and reason for being here today," the corrections officer asked.

"Dallas Police Homicide Detective Lance Harris, and I am here to speak to death row inmate, Johnny Watson."

The corrections officer had a brief smile on his face before he corrected his expression.

"Detective, we are familiar with Watson." He hit the button to release the locked gate.

He walked down another long hall and greeted two correctional officers in charge of the visitation area.

"Sir, we have you set up at the very end of the hall, and we will have it blocked off so you can have privacy. Once you are ready, we will bring in inmate Watson."

"Thank you." Another clanging sound as the door was opened.

Harris walked into a long hall of rooms with sitting areas isolated by wall blocks. A telephone was hanging on the wall of each cage.

He passed only a couple of people on the phone. He stopped at the last desk cubicle. There was a small desk where he dropped his folder with background information, and waits, wondering what was going to happen.

Watson was waiting in his sixty-square foot cell for the guards to come get him. He looked out one of the two window slits in the prison cell door. He saw two guards walking towards his cell. He stood back.

"Johnny Watson, please stand back," as the loud clanging sound indicated the cell door being opened.

The guards were heavily armed as they escorted Watson down several long, stark white hallways to the visitation area.

Watson was taken down the caged booths to the very end. He turned and stared at Detective Harris. Hatred jumped up from his gut and compromised his breathing.

He took deep breaths as he sat down at the desk. The two men stared at each other as Watson picked up the phone.

"I have nothing to say to you."

Harris, holding the phone, sat down and faced Watson.

"I am innocent, you asshole. And I will be out of here soon."

"Chill. We've been investigating three recent homicides, and I want to know who you are working with on the outside. What you say stays between us."

"Fuck you. I have nothing to say."

Harris figured this was going to be a waste of time, but he had to cover all angles.

"If you help us with who you are working with on the outside, that is carrying on these murders, I can help you get moved somewhere else."

"Guards—Guards remove me now!" Watson shouted.

Lance pointed at Watson. "You will regret this, you bastard." He turned and walked down the hallway to the exit.

CHAPTER FOURTEEN

Claire found Chandler getting coffee at the television station cafeteria.

"Hey, what's up?"

"Not much, just getting my camera equipment together."

"I'm looking for a story angle. What if we interview the jogger who found the body? Then, you know, we need to go by the Campbell's and see if they have a comment. Have you heard anything new?" Claire asked. Chandler shook his head no.

"I can't get ahold of Harris or Pierce. Everyone is out, and it is frustrating. At least we know there wasn't another murder. Let me go make the calls."

Claire turned to look for Hillary, the Assignments Editor.

Chandler sipped his coffee and watched her walk, the sway of her hips and the way she shook her hair loose. He reminded himself to be patient.

Claire saw Hillary coming out of the News Director's office.

"Hey, Hillary."

Hillary stopped and waited for Claire to catch up. They walked towards the middle of the newsroom and to Hillary's desk.

"Do you have a contact for the jogger who found Jessica's

body?"

"Not only do I know who it is, I am friends with her, Allison Johnson. Let me give her a call. What time do you want to interview her?"

"I'm ready whenever she's available. I'm waiting to hear back from one of the detectives or Pierce. I'll be at my desk. I have to call the Campbell's and see if they will interview with me. That's all I have now unless something breaks."

"Let's hope it does." Hillary picked up her phone to make the call.

Claire headed over to her desk, dodging the business and education reporters in an intense discussion about the economy.

Claire plopped in her chair and turned on her computer to check her e-mail. She checked the local newspaper website for anything new. Meanwhile, she called directory assistance, got the Campbell's home number and made the call.

Claire dreaded hearing the phone ringing, and a part of her hoped no one answered, but it had to be done.

"Campbell residence."

"Good morning. This is Claire McKenzie. I am a reporter with KABC here in Dallas. I know this is a horrible time, but I wanted to see if they would like to talk."

Total silence.

Claire caught her breath as she waited.

"Ms. McKenzie. The Campbells are in the process of planning their daughter's funeral. There may be a comment later today for the media through their attorney. At this time they have no plans to talk to any media. They are grieving and wish to be left alone."

"I understand completely. Please tell them I am so sorry. Thank you."

As Claire started to hang up, she faintly heard the man on the phone say 'wait.'

"Yes, sir."

"Mrs. Campbell would like you to know she appreciates the care you displayed after interviewing Jessica's friends, and she appreciates that you took to heart that Jessica was not a wild person and would never leave with anyone she didn't know."

"Thank you for the kind words. I appreciate it very much."

Silence.

Claire hung up the phone and fought the tears forming in her eyes. At that moment, Hillary walked up and handed her a note.

"Are you okay?"

"I just talked to someone at the Campbell house. They aren't doing interviews. They're preparing for Jessica's funeral. They did thank me for the way I portrayed Jessica in yesterday's story and interviews with her friends, that she wasn't bad. Sometimes I wonder how long I can last, turning on and off the emotions that you have to do in this job."

"That's the only way you survive, Claire. You turn it off."

"Sometimes you have to feel. Is that Allison's contact information?"

"What time does she want to interview?"

"The same Starbucks as yesterday. It's a little after nine, and she'll meet you there at ten."

"On my way," Claire grabbed her purse, notepad and laptop. She wanted everything with her.

She headed out of the newsroom, down the hall to the photographer's office in the production area, close to KABC's anchor and news desk.

Claire found Chandler working on his laptop.

"You ready to roll? Allison is the jogger's name, and she's going to meet us at the Starbucks off of Greenville at ten."

"Let's go." Chandler grabbed Claire's arm to lead her out the back to his car.

"Why aren't we taking a news van?"

"I think we need to be incognito sometimes."

Claire was too upset to protest.

As they snaked through the Dallas morning traffic, Chandler kept looking over at Claire wondering what was going on. Claire was looking straight ahead, no expression on her face. Finally, she spoke.

"I feel physically ill about what happened, and for her family and friends. How can someone be so evil to do anything to another human being?"

"Hey, she should've known better than to leave with someone she didn't really know."

"What's wrong with you? No one deserves to ever die like that."

Claire climbed into her pouting mode, wondering how Chandler could sometimes be such a jerk. It was the first time she really felt hate towards him.

As Chandler pulled his Viper up to the sidewalk in front of the Starbucks, Claire started to open the door.

"Whoa, wait a minute."

"I'm going to look for Allison and get her comfortable before all the camera equipment starts flying in and I have to approve it with the manager."

Claire slammed the door.

"Shit, what's her problem?" He drove into the side parking lot and parked his car. He got out, unloaded his equipment and headed to the door.

Inside, Claire went straight for the counter.

"Can I speak to the manager, please?"

She waited there for a minute, then out popped Brad Quinton from behind the counter. He came around the side towards Claire.

"It's so good to see you, Claire. I'm sorry about Jessica. She was a nice young lady with everything ahead of her. So sad. I would talk to her sometimes when she came in here in the early morning hours to get organized. What can I do for you?"

"Do you mind if I do a quick interview in the corner over there?"

At that moment Claire felt a tap on her shoulder and turned.

"Hi, you must be Allison." She held out her hand.

"Yes, I am. It's nice to meet you."

Claire turned back to Brad.

"Allison was the jogger who found Jessica. Do you mind if I interview her over in the corner?"

"Of course. Anything that might lead us to the maniac who killed Jessica."

"Thanks, Brad. I will talk to you later."

Claire pointed in the direction of the large table in the back. She and Allison moved and sat down.

"Are you doing okay?" Claire asked.

"Not really," Allison said, looking as if she was about to cry.

"It was horrible to find her. I knew the media would want to interview me, and I told Hillary yesterday I would feel up to it today."

"Oh, here's my photographer, Allison. This is Chandler."

"Nice to meet you." She shook his hand.

"Nice to meet you. I'll just be a moment setting up the camera."

As Allison and Claire talked, Chandler set up his stand, hooked the camera on top, and made sure it was steady before he set the microphone on its stand in front of Allison.

"Ready."

Claire smiled, trying to help Allison relax. She knew it always makes people nervous to sit down and talk with a reporter.

"You'll do fine. Allison, tell me what you saw two days

ago."

"I always run in the morning, early morning like between five and six, so I can have plenty of time to get ready for work. I don't have to tell you where I work, do I?"

"No, that's not necessary. How did you happen to see Jessica?"

"For just a moment I glanced over, and I saw what looked like a hand. I thought, 'Oh boy, Allison, you're really imagining things.' So I kept running for another half a mile. Then I stopped and thought, 'You know, I'd better go back and check it out for sure. As I was running back, I passed two joggers, both male. One ran off of the path as soon as I passed him. I then came around the corner, and that's when I saw the hand again. I started walking, and when I leaned over and lifted up the tree limb, oh god." Her voice broke in a sob, and a tear slid down her cheek. "That's when I saw her body. It was horrible. Then I pulled my phone out of my knapsack and called 911."

"Then what happened?"

By now, Allison had pulled herself back up. "The police arrived fast. I waited in one of the police cars, then the detective interviewed me about what I'd seen."

"Did you know Jessica?"

"I didn't, but it doesn't matter. It could've easily been my friend or your friend. I'm so sorry for her family."

"Thank you, Allison. I know it's hard to do this."

"I just want them to catch him. Can I ask your photographer a question?"

"Sure."

Both women turned to Chandler. He stopped gathering the cable and waited for Allison.

"Did I see you at the park that morning? Do you go jogging there? You look familiar, kind of like one of the guys that ran past me."

Chandler laughed, "Oh, I wish I could say I was that

disciplined, but no, I was in the sack."

Neither of them laughed. Allison stood, so did Claire.

"Thanks again for the interview." Claire handed the jogger her card with her cell phone number on it.

"Call me if you think of anything."

Allison nodded and walked away.

Chandler picked up the camera equipment and followed Claire out of Starbucks. Everyone stared as they made their way through the store, but no one said anything to them. Claire held the door open.

As they stepped out on the sidewalk, Chandler motioned to the side parking lot. They headed that way. Chandler clicked his car lock, and Claire got in.

Chandler loaded the equipment into the backseat, got in, buckled his seat belt and started his Viper, looking over at Claire.

"What do you think? You want to have an early lunch in case something happens this afternoon?" Chandler asked as he backed out of the parking lot.

"Why do you think she thought she recognized you?"

"Claire, I have no idea. Lots of guys are six-foot-one and my size. What about lunch?"

"I can't. I'm supposed to meet Eric. I'm telling him again to leave me alone and I want him to go on with his life. He's not getting the message, so I am trying again. I am going to meet him at that Starbucks off of Mockingbird. Do you mind dropping me off? I can call you on your cell to come get me when I finish."

"Okay." Chandler turned and headed east on Mockingbird.

They traveled in silence.

"Right there," Claire pointed.

Chandler stopped. Claire jumped out to the sidewalk. "I'll call you," closing the passenger door and walking away.

Chandler watched her. Her short dress was tight and it hit

him hard. *Patience*, he reminded himself as he cut off a car that honked as he shot out into the left lane.

Eric was standing, looking out of the Starbucks window when he saw Chandler pull up to the curb, dropping off Claire and driving away.

Claire checked her cell phone and walked inside. She passed a couple, arm in arm, trying to carry their coffee as they snuggled. Claire needed to make this fast so she could get back to work on her story.

Eric moved to the back of the shop and was acting like he was bouncing off the walls, appearing to be excited to see Claire. He kissed her on the lips and grabbed her hand, trying to pull her around the circular booth next to him. Claire jerked back, and Eric tried to contain his temper. For the next fifteen minutes they talked about work and nothing in general.

Claire changed her temperament. "Eric, I am over-whelmed right now and I can't commit to a relationship. I want to stay friends, but you go do whatever you want to do or go out with whomever you want, and we'll just be friends."

"I understand."

Claire was shocked. Maybe this wouldn't be as bad as she first thought.

"I need to get my books and CDs we were looking at a couple of weeks ago. Can you just leave them in the mailbox? I would appreciate it."

She stood.

"Not a problem," he followed close behind Claire as she headed to the door.

Claire called Chandler as she walked out the front door, tagged behind by Eric.

"I'm ready."

"Be right there."

Claire didn't know Chandler was in the parking lot, watching the whole scene.

Claire turned to tell Eric goodbye as Chandler pulled up. Eric gave her another kiss and hugged her tight.

Claire was trying not to get sick, especially when he pushed himself into her dress. Did Eric not hear what she said? She prayed Chandler would appear.

He was trying to hold his temper and not get out and smack the guy in the face.

Claire yanked back away from Eric. She ran for the car, afraid she was going to vomit.

Chandler was trying to contain his anger.

He asked her why they looked so cozy when he thought she was breaking up with him.

She didn't reply.

"It looked that way to me," Chandler said.

Claire worried that Eric didn't get the message after all. She couldn't think about that now. They needed to get to the police station to interview the Communications Officer. She still couldn't get through to Lance at the station and had been leaving several messages. She had his cell phone number, but she didn't want to use it except in an emergency.

Chief Lewis was looking for Lance. He called Reid.

"I want to see him now. Why didn't I get an update this morning?"

Reid spilled out where Lance was and what they planned last night.

"Sir, Lance is out in the field interviewing sources."

"You bring him in from the field. That's why he is chief deputy and he has detectives under him."

CHAPTER FIFTEEN

Lance walked out of the Huntsville State prison. He wished he could take a shower. Watson would not reveal anything, but he did confirm Lance's worst fear. It was either his accomplice out there or he was feeding someone information.

As Lance drove north on Interstate Highway 45 heading back to Dallas, he flipped open his phone for messages. One call from the Chief, two from Reid and one from Claire.

He needed to touch base with his partner first.

"What's up?"

"On your way back?" Reid asked.

"Yeah, Watson was a total asshole, declared his innocence, all that crap. I need to check on the release of an inmate next to him to see what's up there. They're going to fax a copy of all of his visitors the last six months. Otherwise, it was a total waste of time. What's the latest information on Eric?"

"You're not going to like this. He was charged with sexual assault his senior year at SMU, two years ago. Charges were later dropped when the girl refused to press charges or testify. My source in the DA's office said she wasn't the first. They couldn't figure out if he paid the girls to be quiet or what. They said he's nothing but scum and they'd do anything to get charges to stick. Haven't heard anything lately, but they believe he's dealing with an underground prostitution network. Hard to get."

"I want that bastard under surveillance immediately. I don't know how, but let's figure it out and get those charges for the DA. He is one of our suspects in the Smiley Face murders, starting now."

"That'd be the only way to get surveillance approved. What about Claire?"

"I'll talk to her after I get back in town and get some things taken care of. Any news?"

"Chief is looking for you. I told him you were out in the field checking out witnesses and you were checking with a friend in the FBI's Office. I told him I called you and you didn't answer. He's pissed, but then people were waiting outside his office, so you're clear until this afternoon."

"I'll be back later this afternoon. I'll check in with him first. What else do you have?"

"Ryan is following up on any connection between our victims."

"Call me if anything else comes up." Lance ended the call.

His worst fears were confirmed. Lance wanted Eric put under immediate surveillance as a suspect.

As he drove, Lance needed to call his buddy, Jake, with the FBI. He waited for the connection.

"Jake, Lance here."

"Hey, looks like you have your hands tied behind your back. Anything I can do?"

"If we don't get any solid leads soon, I'm calling you in."

"Chief won't like it."

"Yeah, but finding this asshole is more important than playing the dance. I just left Huntsville. Talked with Watson. Of course he still says he was framed and is innocent. I don't know. I'm starting to have doubts, not that Watson isn't involved somehow, but with the latest victim showing up with a smiley face sticker. I don't believe in coincidences. At least I know he's not going anywhere while our investigation continues."

"Let me know."

"Sure."

It'd been niggling in the back of his mind all morning, even if Lance didn't want to face it. Could Watson be innocent? No. Our guys covered all of the bases. We have the right man all along. His heart took a dive and pain hit into his gut.

He couldn't be wrong. They couldn't be wrong.

Doubts crept up. No! That bastard has an outside connection, and I'm going to find it, dammit!

Lance told himself he shouldn't, but after work he was going to go by Claire's house, just to make sure everything looked safe.

He sped up as he crossed along the bridge that flowed into downtown Dallas. For a brief moment on the left, the buildings and streets looked more like a war zone, then less than twenty seconds later he saw Fair Park and the Dallas Municipal Dump on the right.

Next he was surrounded by upscale condominiums and specialty stores. Oh, that's living in the city, Lance thought as he exited to Main Street off of the freeway, making the light as he turned left towards the Dallas Police headquarters.

It was about three in the afternoon as he parked and headed to the backdoor.

Lance hoped the Chief was still tied up, so he could get to his office and check out what was going on with his team.

It appeared hectic as Lance walked into the homicide division offices, opening his office door, he stepped up to his desk, looked up and waved through his window at Reid. He checked his messages. The preliminary autopsy report may be in.

Lance stuck his head in the office door.

"Reid, tell Missing Persons to let us know if any reports

come in of missing women ages eighteen to forty-five in the last six months to today," Lance said. "Tell them to call me or you, no matter what time of day or night, ASAP. It looks like we have a preliminary report. I'm calling Spencer on the autopsy now."

Claire was back at the television station writing her story and Chandler was busy getting shots ready for the final edit. He had pulled file video from the murder scene from the other day, and he was waiting for Claire. He watched her through the hall glass as she worked on her computer. She would come to him someday, after she rid herself of all of these other jerks, he told himself. She'd be all his one day. He just needed to be patient and wait.

Claire moved her mouse to save and send her story to the computer in editing. She jumped up from her desk and walked across to the room packed with reporters, editors and producers.

There was a certain humming noise that is typical in the newsroom for this time of day, a slight electric feeling as everyone pushed to make the newscast deadline.

"Hey there, are you ready?" Claire asked. "I never tell you enough how I rely on you, and I appreciate all you do for me. I have just a few changes we need to add. Video, too."

Chandler just smiled and took her arm, gently pulling her down on the chair, closer to him.

"Let's get your audio cut. It's getting close to news time."

The meeting with the Chief went smoother than Lance expected. He made the Chief think he let the FBI know it was the Chief's idea to get a profile. He was back in his office trying to get caught up on everything that happened while he was gone.

Lance switched the six newscast on. He was waiting to watch Claire. He was also following up on his paperwork when the newscast came on. He watched with interest,

Claire's interview with the female jogger. Once it was over he called Reid.

"We need a bulletin released. I want both of those joggers interviewed by tomorrow morning." He stood, stretching his back. He walked over to his office window and stared at the Dallas skyline.

Women weren't safe out there tonight, and that included Claire.

"Where are you, you bastard? I'll find you this time, and if the chance comes up, I'll kill you."

The six newscast had just wrapped up. Dwight tossed the close to Claire so she could tease her story for the ten newscast. Competition was fierce between the local television stations. High ratings meant commercial money, honor and recognition, and it was up to television reporters, like Claire, to get the exclusive story.

Claire took off her microphone and stood up from the anchor desk. "Dwight, where's Melissa? It's not like her not to show up and not call."

"Something came up at school I bet. You know how those college kids are."

"I don't have a good feeling. I am going by her apartment on my dinner break," Claire said as she stepped down away from the anchor desk.

"Whatever floats your boat," Dwight said, laughing to himself.

The other production staff on the set who were getting the equipment ready for the ten newscast didn't say a word. A few rolled their eyes. Dwight was definitely amused by himself.

She walked away down the hall, trying to contain her anger. What a jerk, she thought. I bet Dwight doesn't know the names of more than two people at the station. He is so into himself.

Claire went into the editing booth to add her name to the

story. There was not much at six that was different, so she was going to concentrate on a new angle at ten. When she finished, she headed to her Hummer, feeling like things weren't good. Maybe she should try Lance again? Claire was standing in the parking lot on her cell phone.

"Detective Harris."

"Lance, it's Claire."

"What do you need? I have a murder investigation underway." Lance shook his head, not meaning to sound so blunt. It was shaking him up having Claire around again.

"Melissa didn't show up for work today. She's an intern, and she's really driven and would never skip out." Claire started to feel panicked.

Lance had that cop radar going off that something was wrong.

"I am on my way to her apartment," she said.

"Claire don't, I'll go. What's her address?"

"5432 Claremont, Apartment 22. It's close to the SMU campus. I'll meet you there." She hung up.

Lance tried to call Claire back as he motioned for Reid and headed for the door, but it went to voicemail.

Claire made it to Melissa's apartment first. She had that women's intuition kick in that something was wrong-when your radar in the back of your neck goes off. Claire always believed in reacting to your instincts and being careful and on full alert.

Claire cried out when she reached for the door and it was unlocked. Melissa was steadfast about security. She'd never leave her door unlocked.

Claire opened the door and pushed her way in, and the smell slapped her in the face. She looked into the kitchen and froze. She gasped and her mouth dropped open.

Melissa was spread out on the kitchen floor. Blood everywhere. In a trance, Claire went to her friend, her co-worker.

She bent down to check Melissa's pulse.

That was when she saw the smiley face sticker on Melissa's shirt.

The next thing Claire knew, there were shouts. "Police." Shouts surrounded her and made her head spin even more.

It sounded like the Dallas Police SWAT team had come in yelling. Claire looked up to see Lance, and everything turned black as she fainted.

"Ms. McKenzie, how are you feeling?" the paramedic asked her. She was lying on top of a cot out in the apartment parking lot where they'd carried her after she fainted.

Lance was kneeling down beside her, holding on to her.

Claire grabbed his arm, "Melissa," was all she could say to Lance.

Lance was holding her hand and put his other hand on her forehead.

"She's in shock, sir. I think we should take her to the hospital," the medic said.

"Okay," Lance leaned over her. "I'll be there as soon as I can," he whispered in her ear.

He released her as the gurney was moved to the ambulance.

Claire screamed, "No, Lance I want to stay."

Everyone ignored her as the paramedics quickly began loading her into the ambulance and Lance headed back to the murder scene.

Where is Chandler? Claire was thinking. Oh, my god, Melissa. She covered her face and softly cried as she was hoisted into the ambulance.

If the truth was known, Lance was glad to have Claire going somewhere safe.

Lance turned and walked back to Melissa's apartment. Lance took in the crowd that had gathered outside, took a sweep with his eyes, wondering if the killer was in the crowd, something not that unusual. The asshole would want to gloat over the attention. Behind him, Spencer, the County Medical Examiner, came up with his assistant, Brandon, carrying his bag to gather evidence and figure out how the young lady was killed.

"Harris, what's up?"

"The news lady, Claire McKenzie, came to check on her friend and co-worker. The door was unlocked and she found her on the floor in the kitchen. There's blood everywhere."

"Was that Claire in the ambulance?"

"They say she's in shock," Lance replied as they climbed the stairs.

"There is a strange smell inside," Spencer said, as he headed toward the kitchen.

Detectives were everywhere, going through Melissa's apartment, dusting for fingerprints, footprints, securing the scene, trying to find anything that might lead them to the killer.

Davis and Ryan were knocking on doors around Melissa's apartment to see if anyone saw or heard anything.

Lance watched as Spencer and his assistant, Brandon, bent down to look at Melissa's body. He lifted the 'smiley face sticker' off of her blouse and looked up at Lance as he put it in an evidence bag.

"Fingerprint, we'll see."

"What do you think?"

"Right now I'd say she was stabbed several times and she fought like a tiger. Look at her hands." He lifted them up towards Harris. "She may have injured our suspect. I won't know until I get her back for the autopsy what else was done to her."

"Claire said she didn't show up for work today and didn't call. She was supposed to be at the station by one this afternoon. Everyone just blew it off to her being a college student, except for Claire. She called me after the six newscast and said she was going to check on her friend. I arrived seconds after her and heard her scream as I was coming up the stairs."

"That's tough. Let's see what else we have."

"Time of death?" Harris asked.

"I'll have to let you know. We will be moving the body soon," Spencer said. "Brandon, can you get the equipment please?"

"Yes, sir."

CHAPTER SIXTEEN

Lance was standing quietly in the background, observing the scene as Spencer got the body ready to be removed. Shaun, Ryan and Davis, gloves on, continued to meticulously go through not only the kitchen, but Davis had moved into the living room and her office area where her computer was.

There was a container in the middle of the floor full of evidence bags, anything the detectives hoped might bring them a clue. Lance started to move toward Davis to remind him to wait for the computer specialists, then he looked in the kitchen again and noticed Reid looking out the back window.

He didn't like the expression he saw on his fellow detective's face. Something was wrong.

"Chief, come here and look at this—it may be big," Ryan called out to Lance.

He abandoned his question for Reid for the moment and made his way to Ryan, then bent down to see what Ryan was looking at.

It appeared to be a small kitchen knife lodged between the end of the cabinet and the trash can. It had blood on it.

"Dr. Wyatt said it looked like she fought like a tiger against her attacker. It could be her knife that she dropped during the attack."

Lance slyly smiled. "Let's hope to hell we've got him."

Lance stood and called out to Shaun.

"Get Tim and canvass the neighborhood. See if anybody has seen her or seen anyone with her."

"Yes sir." Shaun headed for the door.

"Reid," Lance yelled across the room. "I want to talk to the news director and his employees."

"Right on it." Reid walked to the front door outside to find the Channel Two news crew.

Melissa's once modernly furnished apartment looked like a war zone. Lamps from the tables in the den had been knocked off. It was like someone tried to grab the fireplace poker and knocked over magazines and decorative items Melissa had on the fireplace hearth, and two chairs in the kitchen had been turned over. Lance was so angry, but he had to push it away and concentrate on catching the killer. He needed to calm himself and concentrate on how he planned to address the Channel Two news crew.

Claire woke up, fear running through her veins. She was in a strange bed, feeling odd sensations, not knowing where she was. Seconds later it all swarmed back into her head and she screamed. In rushed a nurse with a young doctor not far behind.

The doctor grabbed her hand and pushed her hair out of her face.

"Ms. McKenzie, are you okay? How do you feel?"

Claire voiced a whisper, "Yes, Doctor." She failed to hold her tears at bay.

"I can't believe my friend's dead." She buried her face in his hands.

The doctor and the nurse waited for her to compose herself. Claire looked up, tears streaming down her face. "I am fine, Doctor. I just want to go home."

Out of the corner of her eye, she noticed a large shadow hovering in the doorway. *Lance.* Claire's heart plummeted to her stomach, but in a different way than when she'd found Melissa.

He reached his hand out.

"Doctor, I am Dallas Detective Lance Harris, and I'm here to get Claire safely home."

"Good evening, I am Dr. Finney. She'll be fine with rest. She may be tired from the tranquilizer she received when she arrived, so she should not be driving for at least twenty-four hours."

"I'll make sure of that."

"Let me get Ms. McKenzie's discharge paperwork. I'll be right back." Dr. Finney and the nurse walked out of the room.

"Hey there, you doing better?" Lance put his arms around Claire, holding her close. Claire melted into his chest, thinking she never wanted this moment to end. For a couple of minutes they held each other until they heard Dr. Finney clear his throat as he walked back into the hospital room. First he handed Claire her purse and told her it had been kept in a safe and her cell phone was inside her purse.

"Here, Ms. McKenzie, just sign here and here and you may leave. I have included instructions for your recovery. You call me if anything comes up. I've included my cell number."

Lance had to turn away. Nothing like the doctor being so obvious. Lance then stepped back so Claire could lean over and sign the paperwork.

"Thank you, Dr. Finney."

"I feel like I know you, watching you on television every night."

At that, Lance rolled his eyes. He thought the nurse usually brought the discharge paperwork for the patient to sign.

"Thank you for watching, Dr. Finney."

Claire wobbled as soon as her feet hit the floor, and both men reached for her. Dizziness swamped her form, and she almost fell back onto the bed.

Claire laughed, "I do feel a little woozy."

Lance took her elbow and guided her toward the door. The lights were too bright as they walk out into the hallway. The nurse came up behind them with a wheelchair.

"Here, she needs to be taken out in the wheelchair."

"Oh gosh, no. I am fine."

"Hospital policy, Ms. McKenzie."

"Go ahead and sit," Lance admonished.

She pouted as she turned to sit down in the wheelchair.

"Here, I'll take her," Lance told the nurse, and he didn't listen to the woman's protest as he took off for the exit.

Since they were on the second floor, Lance maneuvered to the handicap stairwell. Down they went, and the exit doors automatically opened and out into the warm night they went.

"Nothing like a little special attention from Dr. Finney."

Claire laughed and for a moment her pain disappeared.

They reached Lance's truck and Claire stepped out of the wheelchair as Lance clicked the lock.

Claire sat in the passenger seat and leaned her head back as she watched Lance walk back to the side door to give the intern the wheelchair before trotting back to his truck to get in. "Claire, you doing better?"

"Yes. I just want to go home." She couldn't help but watch him as he returned the wheelchair. He looked hot no matter what he was dressed in.

"On our way." Lance started the engine, backed out, and hit the gas, sending them out of the hospital parking lot.

Neither spoke on the ride home to Claire's house.

What was there to say? If Lance had any new information about Melissa she knew he would tell her.

Lance's mind was reeling with everything that happened. The investigation was stalled and now Claire's friend was dead because of that. *Where are you, you bastard?* He thought as he headed down the road.

Lance pulled his truck into Claire's driveway and stopped. "I'm going to stay here tonight. I'll sleep on the couch."

"That's not necessary, Lance."

"It is. I don't want you alone."

"Just get the son-of-a bitch." Claire slowly got out of the truck. Lance followed behind up the front porch steps. Claire unlocked her front door and flipped on the porch lights. Lance gestured for her to stand by the front door. He pulled out his gun.

"Let me check everything. Stay here," Lance said as he raised his gun and walked toward the dining room and kitchen.

"Sure."

Claire waited as Lance slowly climbed the stairs. She could hear him walking across the bedroom, then opening the back porch door. Moments later, he returned back down the stairs.

He walked into the family room where Claire had turned on a lamp.

"I wish I could have a glass of wine, but I don't think that's a good idea," Claire said.

"No, I don't think so," he said.

"What's going on with the investigation?" Claire moved into that unemotional mode to be able to operate, her work mode. She couldn't bring herself to say Melissa's name because she'd start crying.

"Detectives Ryan and Shaun are doing interviews. Forensics is still there."

"Shouldn't you be there?"

Lance hesitated, he felt guilty dumping the investigation all on Sanchez, but he didn't want Claire's photographer taking her home. There was something not right there, and he was going to find out what.

Reid understood and told him to check in for the latest.

"I should be there, but I need to be here with you."

Tears formed in her eyes, even though she didn't say anything.

Lance's chest clutched as he looked down and saw Claire's pain.

"I'm so sorry, Claire. I will get this bastard." He tugged her to him, wrapping his arms around her.

"I'll stay on the couch tonight."

Claire stared but didn't say anything.

"Why don't you go get ready for bed," Lance said.

Claire swayed, feeling dizzy and devastated about what had happened to her co-worker, her friend. She knew she should call her family, but she couldn't deal with everything tonight and all of the questions she knew they would have for her.

"Thanks for coming to get me."

"No problem. Go to bed. I'll be here."

Claire headed upstairs without looking back.

Lance sat down at the kitchen table to call Reid. He might as well make himself comfortable.

"What's the latest?"

"Forensics is still busy. Her parents are here, getting ready to talk with me. I've been here trying to take it all in. Ryan is staying with them, trying to get what information he can before I talk to them. We need to interview her friends."

"Have you heard from the Chief?"

"No, he had some social event tonight."

Lance's anger started to surface. "That bastard. Here we have a serial killer loose and he's partying?"

"Well, you know how it is. All politics," Reid said. "Anyway, I need to get back to this. Stay with Claire. We're holding the fort down, but I'll call you with anything pressing."

"Got it."

Claire was standing at her bedroom door, listening to Lance talk about the case.

Now, she could hear him moving around downstairs. Was he getting settled in her living room?

Claire pulled out her cell phone and called Jennifer in the newsroom.

"Hey Jennifer, it's Claire. What's the latest?"

"Claire, my goodness, are you okay? You need to be resting. We're hanging in as best as we can," Jennifer said.

"I'll see you sometime tomorrow. Let me know if anything changes. You are the best. Thanks for being there for me."

"Thanks for being who you are. We miss you. Get some rest and we'll see you tomorrow."

Claire disconnected the call. She dreaded tomorrow. How was she going to face the day, knowing what had happened to Melissa? She'd have to go see Melissa's parents tomorrow.

She walked to her bed, slipped under the covers and turned off the light. She couldn't sleep. All she could think about was Melissa, and she cried as she turned over.

How could she work tomorrow? She didn't want to tune in to Valerie, about whom the News Director sent her a text, letting her know she was doing the story for the morning newscast.

Claire knew she had to get some sleep—she was missing something. There was a clue there that might help. Did the doctor give her a valium? She couldn't remember as she turned over on her side and cried herself to sleep.

Lance wanted Claire, but he knew she needed her sleep to recover, and he needed to keep his mind on the investigation. Maybe he could crawl in her bed and just hold her. No, that wouldn't happen. *Keep it together, man.* Lance stretched out on the couch and tried to sleep, but it didn't happen for a long time.

He was hidden behind the mesquite bush on the side of Claire's house, watching and waiting. He watched as Detective Harris went inside with her. He noticed that Harris locked the door. Tonight's not the night. He turned and started slowly jogging down the street, on the dark side of the night lights, to his car parked around the block.

CHAPTER SEVENTEEN

The next morning there was still activity going on at Melissa's apartment when Lance drove up.

It had been hard leaving Claire this morning, but she knew he had to go and she promised to be careful and to keep all doors locked.

He saw Ryan walking an older couple to a Cadillac. It must be Melissa's parents, John and Patsy Wilkes. As he jogged over, he noticed Reid interviewing with the news media. It looked like a circus.

"I'm Detective Harris," he says softly as he reached for Mrs. Wilkes' hand.

"Patsy, please," she burst into tears and crumbled to the ground as her husband grabbed her to keep her from falling.

"I'm sorry, Detective. I need to get her home. I've called our family physician to come over. I'm John Wilkes."

"Mr. Wilkes, we will do everything we can. Can I come by later?"

"Certainly."

At that moment, Harris spotted one of his female detectives walking with a young girl, around seventeen or eighteen years old. Ryan and Tim helped bring the girl over. She'd been crying, but the resemblance was clear. She was Melissa's sister. They looked nearly identical.

As the parents continued towards the car, Harris walked up and introduced himself.

"I'm Detective Lance Harris, and I am so sorry. I'll need to talk to you later, if that's okay."

"I am Melissa's sister, Shannon. I will be available."

As Ryan and Tim walked Shannon to her car, the female detective stopped next to Lance.

"Did she say anything?" he asked.

"Only that she told Shannon that she felt like she was being followed the last couple of days. Melissa is the one who apparently set up the interviews with Jessica's friends for Claire McKenzie. Do you remember seeing that story on the ten newscast? It was very effective. After that is when Melissa started feeling someone was watching her."

"Good work. I'll be in touch, Detective," as he walked toward Reid who was finishing up with the last forensic assistant.

"Anything I need to know about what the media was asking?" Lance asked.

"No, I was great at the 'no comment' answer."

"Should we head to the station?"

"Yes, call everyone in. Let's see what we have and make assignments. See you in ten."

Lance reached the police station first. He walked in, and strangely enough, it was quiet as he went to the conference room, turned the light on and sat down to look at his notes.

"Spencer there?"

"Sir, he's in the middle of the preliminary. I'll have him call you back."

"Anything he can give me," shutting his cell phone, tired and angry, trying to ignore the mixed emotions assaulting his head.

As he stared at the board with the information about Jessica, he heard commotion in the hallway. When the detectives reached the conference room, no one said a word.

"Glad you could join us. We need a woman's assessment since we don't have jack shit," Lance said to FBI Agent Whitney Walker.

"This is FBI Agent Whitney Walker. She'll be assisting us in the investigation." Lance didn't mention that he hadn't told the Chief yet that he had contacted his FBI buddy, Jake, and asked for Walker. Lance felt they needed a woman's perspective involved in the investigation.

"Here's the latest. Melissa was last seen at the local 7-Eleven down the street from her apartment around three yesterday afternoon. The checkout clerk knows her and said she seemed distracted," Reid said.

"I think we need to follow up on her suspicions that she was being followed after she set up the interviews with Jessica's friends for Claire McKenzie," Ryan said.

"I think you're right on that. Wonder if the Smiley Face Killer watched the news crew do the interviews and he decided Melissa was his next target? He's smart, and he is going to plan everything out with precision because he is not going to get caught," Lance paused.

"Later this morning, Reid and I are meeting with the parents at their house. Ryan, Tim, you and Davis come and we'll interview the sister as well. The crime tech team will join us. Her parents said that we could have her computer and whatever we need. At eleven in the morning, KABC has promised to have all of its employees in the studio for us to interview. We have to get something on this guy. This will not continue."

He added, "I want you to look at everything as if it happened to your own family."

The conference room door opened and Spencer walked in.

"Bad news, it was, in fact, the Smiley Face Killer. I know that it's preliminary, but I wanted you to know."

Lance concluded the meeting as everyone filed out of the conference room. Lance went to his office, walked behind his desk and turned on his computer to check messages.

Sanchez leaned inside the doorway. "He has us running all over the place, so we don't have a chance to do background or even get something going."

"He knows us. He is watching us, I can feel it. I have three suspects in mind that I have to have checked out."

"After the media interviews at the station, we're back here," Sanchez said.

Lance agreed and shut down his computer to leave.

Not even five hours later Lance was showering and getting ready to head back to the police station. He tried Claire on her cell phone. No answer.

"Claire, call me, I want to talk to you before we come out to the television station and meet with everyone."

Lance called the station. "Claire, call me." He didn't want to leave a message that he and Sanchez were going to see Melissa's parents.

As Lance entered the station, he saw Curt at the front desk. "Sir, let me know if there is anything I can do."

"Keep the media away." As Lance walked into his office it was quiet again, as detectives worked on their computers or were on the phone. He waved at Sanchez.

"Let's leave in thirty minutes. Anything new?"

"Nothing. We are looking through the Texas Criminal Investigation Database to see if anyone fits the bare description we have so far. Still going through witness testimony from the scene, but nothing jumps out."

Lance slammed his fist on his desk, "Damn. Who knew all three women—someone did, and that's why they are dead," Lance said.

His phone rang and Sanchez walked out of the office to give him privacy.

"Detective Harris."

"Preston here, the Chief wanted to know about an FBI agent and what the hell she is doing here at the station, involved in the investigation."

"FBI Agent Whitney Walker. She has investigated female abduction and murder cases, and I felt we needed a woman's perspective on the case."

"He's not happy."

"Make him happy. I'm trying to catch a killer, and I don't have time to worry about everybody's feelings." Lance slammed down the phone.

Lance grabbed his jacket and headed out the door to meet with Melissa's parents. John Wilkes was from old family money. His grandfather and father had started the Wilkes Real Estate Agency and Brokerage firm.

Ten minutes later, Lance pulled up in front of the white brick mansion on Swiss Avenue in Old Dallas.

Melissa's brother, Craig, was a senior and played football and had plans to go to Texas A&M to continue his football career while going to college. Shannon, her sister, was a sophomore and a cheerleader. Lance had read earlier from the report, that Whitney had researched and written. She had briefly talked with the family yesterday. They said Melissa was thrilled to be at Channel Two, working as an intern, and that she considered Claire a good friend. She was going to be a senior and was living at the sorority house on campus, but she also had an apartment where she was murdered.

As Lance reviewed the report, he thought of Claire. He feared for her safety. Claire had called back earlier, and their conversation had been short.

"I miss you," Claire told Lance.

"I miss you. Claire, you must be careful, all of you ladies. Please understand how dangerous this killer is. Send me a text when you can so I know you're safe. I need to do an interview.

Let's talk later."

As the call ended, Claire closed her eyes to fight back the tears. Lance was her hero. Please find this madman, Claire thought.

Lance wanted to leave right then, go to Claire and hold her forever. It took everything in his gut to turn his attention and focus from Claire and back to the investigation to stop this killer.

Minutes later, Ryan, Shaun, Tim and Davis arrived along with the Dallas Crime Scene team.

"Time to catch this son-of-a-bitch," Harris said as the team all got out of their cars and walked to the front door.

Meanwhile, back in the Channel Two newsroom a sense of shock and fear could be felt. Some of the girls were sitting on the floor in the middle of the newsroom, staring out into space, unable to comprehend what all was happening. It was quiet in a newsroom that was usually buzzing with action. Some reporters sat and stared at their computers. Some tried to work, but it was hard to concentrate with everything that had happened, and no one knew what was ahead.

CHAPTER EIGHTEEN

Claire was trying to keep a positive attitude, but she was stuck in a nightmare and was barely hanging on.

It had been two days since Melissa's murder and not any news on a suspect to report. Claire's not the only one frustrated. The public and local media are demanding the police find the killer. Melissa's funeral is set for tomorrow.

Claire finished re-editing her piece for the ten newscast. She left the phone numbers of her contacts for the assignments editor to follow up before the news to make sure nothing new broke before the newscast went live. Claire would be available for a live shot.

It was almost seven, so she knew she only had a few hours. Claire remembered Eric said he was going to bring her box of things over several days ago, but he hadn't. She hoped it was already on her front porch. She thought about how cold Chandler seemed today when they were talking about Jessica and Melissa.

What's up with that?

Maybe it didn't matter. Nothing did at the moment. She wanted to get home, and she wished that Lance would be there, but she knew he couldn't be. Twenty minutes later Claire pulled in the driveway. She closed the garage door and went in the back, turned and locked it. Her automatic lighting system worked again. She dumped her briefcase and other items on the kitchen table.

She headed for the front door and out to the mailbox. The box from Eric was not on the porch. Back inside she poured herself a glass of wine. She looked out her kitchen window. It was a beautiful setting on the back porch to enjoy the sunset. She was trying.

She jumped when the doorbell rang. Her hand shook as she put her wine glass down as a shiver ran down her spine as she whirled toward the front door.

"It must be all of this about the Smiley Face Killer," she thought to herself as she went to unlock and open the door.

Eric was standing there in his suit and tie, but no box.

"Eric, I told you I needed that today."

"I want to talk to you. I don't want to break up. We've got a good thing going."

"No, Eric," Claire backed away from the door. "We don't have anything going and we never did. Forget it."

"I would like to come inside and talk. Obviously you haven't checked my Facebook."

"I am not even friends with you—I don't even write on my Facebook page because I have a life," Claire screamed. "No, I want you to leave," trying to shut the door.

"That's not the right answer, Claire." Eric pushed his way inside her house.

Claire was scared now.

He had a look in his eyes she'd never noticed before.

She tried to close the door again.

Eric jammed the door all the way open and shoved her backwards. Claire fell to the floor but scrambled to her feet as fast as she could, despite the ache in her rear end. She needed her cell so she could call 911. She didn't look over her shoulder as she fled, even as she heard Eric click the lock on her front door.

Claire knew what was getting ready to happen. Fear made her heart race, her pulse thundered in her heart. She knew what Eric was going to do, and no way in hell was Claire going to let that happen. She tripped, and he made a grab for her, gripping her jacket with enough force the fabric couldn't hold. The tearing sound rocked Claire to her core.

Eric spun her around and with brute strength, ripped the rest of her jacket off. He pinned her to him; she couldn't breathe.

"I know you want me. I'm going to have you. I'll show you how it can be," he whispered in her ear. She tried to fight, but to no avail. His grip was iron on her torso, and she had to force air down so she wouldn't pass out. Her head started to whirl on her, her vision dancing.

Claire lunged toward him. She bit his shoulder as hard as she could. Eric cursed and yanked himself away, but he grabbed at her before she could get away. She cried out for Eric to stop. She saw her chance and took it. Claire kicked him as hard as she could between the legs and ran up the stairs, screaming.

Eric doubled over, but he was still yelling at her.

She didn't look back. Didn't have much time. Claire dashed into her bedroom and clicked the lock. Right before making a run for the balcony, she grabbed the phone from her nightstand. She was trembling so hard she'd plastered her back against the brick wall outside on her balcony, trying to call 911. She could barely speak when the dispatcher came on.

"What is the address of your emergency?"

Claire forced herself to answer when the dispatcher asked what her emergency was.

"Ma'am, where are you now? Are you at a place he can't get to you?" the woman asked.

"He's here and he's trying to attack me," Claire screamed.

"Ma'am, the police are on their way. They'll be there any

moment. Stay on the line with me. Do you know your attacker?"

"Yes," Claire stammered. She slid to the ground, clutching the phone to her heart, and she couldn't stop crying.

She did her best to answer, but then Claire heard someone yell.

"Police!"

Oh, thank God.

CHAPTER NINETEEN

Lance looked down at his watch. It was past time to call it a day. He needed to check on Claire. He put a quick call in to Reid.

"Did you get that surveillance set up on Eric Thomas?"

"Sure did. They should be watching him right now. Ryan's in charge."

Lance called Detective Ryan. He answered, and sounded like he was outside.

"Lance, we lost the guy when we went to interview him. So sorry. It looks like he has two cars and he came home in his BMW and left in a Mercedes. We didn't see any movement in the house."

"Meet me at 9311 Juniper Drive, the address of Claire McKenzie, the television reporter," Lance yelled as he headed for the door. "My gut says she's in trouble. I think he's there."

"On our way."

He jumped in his truck, also registered as an unmarked police car. Everyone standing around stared at him, and he ignored them, uniform cops and detectives alike. Lance took off fast.

He flipped his lights on and wished like hell he had a siren. Three minutes away from Claire's, the 911 call was transmitted. Lance grabbed his radio.

"This is Deputy Chief Harris. I am a few minutes out. This is the home of television news reporter Claire McKenzie." Oh, shit, I knew it, he reacted. Lance was breathing hard and gearing up. He pulled his gun out of his holster because he knew it was jump, run and save Claire no matter what.

He screeched to a halt across the street, grabbed his gun and raced for the door. *There's the Mercedes.* Was he too late?

No. He couldn't be. His gut—and his heart—rejected that idea. He was there, and he'd make sure Claire was safe. She had to be. There was no other option.

Lance heard sirens, but didn't wait to hit the door. *Claire is screaming.* She'd have to forgive him for kicking in her door. The wood shattered as he put his shoulder and hip to it, then a good shove from his booted foot. He didn't see Eric, or Claire, but the screaming was coming from far away. Maybe upstairs?

"Police!" he yelled, then remembered Claire's bedroom was upstairs. Lance took the stairs two at a time, but maintained his grip on his gun, holding it high.

Her bedroom door was hanging off the hinges, and there was still no sign of either one of them, but he could still hear her terror. Lance burst into her room, aiming his weapon as soon he saw the dark figure.

Eric Thomas was trying to get the balcony door open.

Through the sliding glass doors, he could see a very frightened Claire clutching a cordless phone to her ear.

"Freeze. Police," he commanded.

Eric turned around, surprise evident in his expression. Then the bastard smiled.

"Put your hands up now," Lance ordered. "Arms up! Get down on the ground, slowly, asshole. Then, don't you move!" Lance could hear the sound of backup. Boots on the stairs and other cops calling out.

"In here! The bedroom. I have the suspect."

He called out. "Detective Lance Harris."

Five uniformed officers covered him, entering the room in formation.

"Cover me!" Lance ordered. He wanted to cuff this bastard himself.

The officers ordered Eric Thomas to get down on the ground slowly, like Lance had ordered. He whirled the asshole around shoving him against the wall. The slide and click of the metal bracelets made satisfaction roll over him.

"You'd be a dead man now if I wasn't a cop."

Eric didn't speak. He appeared to be calm as the two officers took him from Lance.

He made eye contact with Lance. "You're going to be a man without a job after this. I'm going to have your badge."

Lance lost it and punched Eric in the face, sending him to his knees. He was furious. Reid and Davis raced into the bedroom. The bastard tried to hurt Claire.

Reid grabbed Lance to stop him right when he'd poised his fist for a second hit. Probably a good idea on his partner's part. Lance was angry enough to inflict real damage. He didn't fight his buddy's grip.

"Your career is over," Eric screamed. Blood trickled down his face.

"Don't get too frisky. Everyone saw how you fell down and hit your head on the floor. Get him out of here."

"You broke my nose, you son-of-a-bitch."

Lance pointed at Eric. "I want him questioned for the Smiley Face murders. I want him charged with attempted murder."

Eric smiled. "You'll be hearing from my attorney."

"Yeah, yeah, get this scumbag out of here." He needed to get to Claire.

Lance almost broke the sliding glass doors lock trying to get it open. His heart stuttered and his gut tightened when his gazed zoned in on her.

Claire was rolled up into the fetal position, lying on the ground. He picked her up, wrapping her in his arms and rocking her. She was shaking, but he knew her strength saved her. Crazy, but he was so proud of her. She was strong and would never give up.

"Claire, talk to me. Are you all right? Did he hurt you?" Lance wanted to make her look at him, but she'd curled into his chest. "You are so smart and strong, and Sweetie, you knew what to do." Lance nearly choked. "I'm so proud of you. I promise you, he will never hurt you again," he said as he hugged Claire close. Lance would kill him first.

She didn't speak, but she nodded.

When their gazes collided, big fat tears rolled down her cheeks. Reid appeared out on the balcony. "Lance," he said. "Davis took Thomas to the station. The paramedics are here to check Claire out. And so is her co-worker, Chandler. He wants to see her."

Lance looked up, but he couldn't read his partner's expression. He carefully helped Claire stand.

"Her News Director is here, and other co-workers. I'll tell them to wait."

"I think you should go to the hospital," Lance said as Claire tried to steady herself.

"I don't want this in the news."

"I understand. Eric is a suspect in the Smiley Face murders."

"Do you realize what that will do to my career if this gets out tonight?"

Claire was furious. She could kill Eric, but she wasn't going to let him ruin her career.

"I think he had this whole thing planned to ruin me. He knew I didn't want to see him or be around him at all. If you charge him, it will ruin me, and that's what he wants. I'm begging you. All he did was tear off my jacket and then I ran for my bedroom and out on the balcony. I locked the door to give me time to call 911."

She couldn't stop the tears. Her whole body shook. Claire tried to fight back the sobs. She was getting it together, remembering the family mantra was 'Never give up!'

"Please, go down and let the medics check you. Then go to the hospital. I'll be there with you in a little while."

"Lance, he didn't rape me. He shoved me down and tore off my jacket. But I got away from him. Do what you want, but I don't want any part of it."

"What if he's the Smiley Face Killer, Claire? What about that? And you didn't help us. Can you live with that?"

He was really angry now. "You do your job, and I'll do mine. Right now you need to go get checked out."

"Take my jacket as evidence."

"You're going to the hospital now."

Claire pushed Lance away. "No."

Inside Claire's bedroom, Reid was standing quietly by the bedroom door. Chandler was standing by Claire's bed, staring out on the balcony at Claire and Lance in their heated discussion.

"Why can't I go out there?" He turned, raising the question to Reid.

"Because she's being questioned and it is an active crime scene."

"About what? She was the victim!"

"Sorry, that's all I can say. You'll just have to wait for them. You shouldn't be up here anyway. Go outside."

Chandler returned his stare to the balcony, at Claire and Lance.

Reid had a bad feeling. Something about Chandler wasn't right. He felt it in his gut. Maybe he'd just pushed it to the back of his mind, since he was Claire's co-worker and obviously one of her friends.

But something was not right. Why would Chandler smile, even if it was a small smile?

He could tell looking outside that Claire and Lance were arguing, and then Claire walked to the door and opened it.

Lance turned to watch what would happen.

Claire saw Chandler and walked into his open arms. Reid was watching closely. Lance watched as well as he walked into the house.

"Can't Claire feel something isn't right?" he whispered to Lance.

Claire stepped back after a too tight hug from Chandler.

"Thanks for coming to check on me."

"We were worried when we couldn't get you on your cell phone, and then I heard the address over the police scanner."

"Is Tim downstairs?"

"Yes."

"Let's make some coffee. We have to talk."

"Are you sure you are up to this now? Shouldn't you go to the hospital?"

"I'm fine, just shaken up a little bit. Too much drama for me," Claire said, trying to make light of the situation.

Chandler took Claire's arm and they headed downstairs.

Reid looked at Lance.

Lance was seething with anger.

"I want him checked out now, dammit."

"On it."

"Let's get to the station. I'll tell you what's up on the way,"

In the living room, Claire was surrounded by her co-workers.

She came to him as soon as his boot hit the bottom stair. She reached for his hand.

"Thank you for saving me. I owe you my life."

As they stood to the side, alone from everyone, she looked

up and nodded, taking his hand, holding it. She blew him a kiss and smiled.

"I'll be back at the station within the hour. See ya then."

"You don't have to thank me," Lance said. "I'll be at the station. For now. I'll be back later. I need to talk to you. If you need anything, you call me. Are you sure you're okay?"

"I'll call you."

"I will check in with you in a little while. Where are you going to stay tonight?"

"I'm going to see if I can stay with Hillary."

"Let me know," he eased down closer. "You can stay with me, Claire."

Claire's News Director was already checking out extra security for the news team and production, along with extra security at the television station.

"We're trying to figure out the game plan for the ten newscast, and we don't have much time."

"Think about filing charges." Lance turned toward the front door.

"Claire, we need a statement," Reid said.

"I know. Lance told me. I will be there in a bit."

If it became all about Claire, the suspect could get away. She'd play it on the ten newscast, exclusive and all.

Lance had a decision to make in less than an hour before the ten newscast that would affect them for the rest of their lives.

If Claire didn't press charges, unless they found anything pointing to his involvement in the murders. They could look into domestic violence.

Claire's kitchen was buzzing. Her News Director, Tim Carlson, one of the assistant news directors, along with Chandler, Greg from engineering and Valerie were all crowded around. Everyone was talking at once, throwing out angles.

Should they break in early to guarantee an audience?

"Sure was smart and lucky you were able to call in to 911."

"Okay, this is the deal. I've asked Detective Harris not to file charges."

"Wow, wait a minute, Claire," said her News Director.

"Look, I know Eric, even though we hardly dated. I think Eric did this on purpose to try and harm my career. If Harris files charges, I'll have to go on live at ten. If he doesn't, I am going to wait and see if I can get through this without anyone finding out about me. Valerie needs to go to the police station for a live shot at ten. They are investigating Eric for the Smiley Face murders. That hopefully will be our lead and not me."

"Wait, are you kidding?" Tim said. "Chandler, you and Valerie, on your way. Greg, set up here for a live shot if it happens. Dwight, back at the studio is just going to have to wing it. We have a little more than two hours. Go!"

"I'm staying with Claire," Chandler said. "Greg can go with Valerie."

"Whatever, let's move it guys."

"I'll work on my script just in case, and I'll call as soon as I hear from Harris."

"Good job," Tim said as he patted Claire's back.

"Be ready for your statement. You may not be able to make this go away," he said as he headed towards the front door. He pointed at Greg, who was gathering up cable.

Claire didn't have time for emotions. She left the room and returned with her computer. She had to get ready for the news live shot.

Chandler, who could barely contain his anger, was watching Claire closely.

What did the police think?

The circus begins.

Sitting at the kitchen table with television cables, wires and microphones skimmed all across the floor, Claire's cell phone rang.

"I'm not going to file charges tonight. I am looking at him for the Smiley Face murders. I want you to reconsider after our interview. I'll take your statement in the morning," Lance said.

She breathed a sigh of relief. "Thank you. Valerie is on her way. If you can do an interview with her, that would be great."

"I can't say much. All of the media will find out tomorrow once they come in and do their early morning follow up for overnight crimes. You are going to have to deal with this."

"Tomorrow. I'll deal with it tomorrow."

Chandler was watching Claire, seething with jealously. The way she flipped her hair back as she was talking to that asshole, Harris. *Someday, Claire, you will realize I am the one.* Later on, the ten evening newscast.

"We're looking at Thomas in connection with the Smiley Face Killer," Lance reported to Valerie, live on the ten newscast. Claire watched from her monitor at home.

Tears burned her eyes. He had left her out of it. Protected her from the media frenzy. For now.

"They have a lot of hard work to do. I pray every day they find him and end the killing."

Chandler looked over at Claire. It made him sick to see that she was sympathizing with Harris.

"He did this for me. I owe him my life."

Since Lance had her back, used her story on the latest on the search for Melissa's murderer, mentioning that he may have been caught tonight.

Claire helped Chandler break down and pack up.

Claire was thinking about Eric, glad for the break, but most importantly, she had to be emotionally ready for tomorrow. She thought, Eric can go to hell. He had better not come anywhere near me again if he wants to live.

Melissa's funeral was also the next day, and it was going

to take all her emotional strength and prayers to get through it.

Police got a search warrant for Thomas's condo.

Claire just wanted it all behind her. She didn't want the incident with Eric to tarnish her image or her career. If she refused to file charges, it would all be dropped.

All she had to worry about was if the other stations figured out the 911 call that led to his arrest had come from her house. They would all report on it immediately. If so, Claire needed to plan what she'd report. She only had a few hours to decide.

It would drop for now, but come up again later on when news stories died down.

That was just how it was done. Stories that did not have a conclusion could be revisited and updated during a slow news period. Always had stories on standby for that.

It was all about ratings.

CHAPTER TWENTY

Hours later, after watching the late news rebroadcast the Smiley Face Killer, News Photographer Jeremy Chandler sipped his scotch and water, and looked out over a beautiful view of downtown Dallas from his hip urban condo.

He paid a load of money every month for his two-bedroom condominium with a veranda porch outside his back door. It was where all of the Uptown people lived, and he blended right in.

The cool people. He was handsome, smart and had a job to die for. He smiled, sipped his drink and remembered those idiots at that newswoman's apartment. He'd watched Melissa; she was savvy. She'd nearly figured it out, but she'd made one mistake.

Melissa knew Jeremy. She worked with him at the television station. Melissa opened the door and had let him into her apartment, turned her back on him, and... oh, well... hanging up the phone had been her last mistake.

Eric was being held in a holding cell, screaming for his attorney.

Lance, Reid and Ryan watched him through a monitor, waiting for the search warrant. The door swung open.

"Here you go, guys," said Corporal Marshall.

Lance snatched the document. "Yes! Let's go."

The three headed out of the viewing room.

Lance yelled back at Marshall, "Corporal, get the forensics team and four additional officers to help."

Racing towards Midtown Dallas in Lance's truck to execute the search warrant fast, his phone rang.

It was the desk sergeant. "Yeah, what's up?"

"Chief, I just received the strangest call from a lady who said she was from New York and she wants to report a missing person. Johnny Watson's twin brother. She claims Watson had something to do with his disappearance."

"From prison? No way. Hold on to that information, and I'll call her after the search warrant. If she calls again give her my cell."

"Will do."

Lance swung the truck into a parking lot of high-end apartments. One squad car was already there.

"Find the Superintendent and tell him we have a warrant for Apartment 69, belonging to Eric Thomas," Lance ordered a uniform cop.

Everyone gathered outside, waiting for someone to let them in. A guy with a Middle Eastern accent accompanied the officer Lance had sent. The Superintendent grudgingly opened the door.

As they swarmed in, guns drawn and making sure the condo was empty, Lance realized they were headed into one fancy apartment.

"Man, what guy decorates his apartment like this?"

Ryan looked around at the leather furniture, latest glass coffee table and end tables, posh, exotic pictures hanging throughout and a bear skin blanket lay carefully across a fancy designed brown leather chair.

Lance was surprised as well, shaking his head as he looked around, rolling his eyes and raising his shoulders. "Amazing."

The place looked clear as the forensics team arrived and

got to work. Reid called from a back bedroom he'd cleared.

"Harris, get your ass over here. You're not going to believe this."

Lance obeyed, trailed by Ryan and Thompson from forensics.

His heart stopped.

The room had been made into an office, was packed full of electronic equipment, including two computers, large monitors, a camera and editing system.

Lance's eyes darted everywhere. He couldn't believe what was covering the walls.

Photos of hundreds of young women. He stopped in his tracks. In the middle of all of the photographs were pictures of Claire, at least six eight-by-ten pictures. And they were framed.

He could distinguish that she didn't know the photographs were being taken. None of them were portrait style. It was more like she hadn't known someone was watching her, or had taken the pictures.

"What've we got here?" Ryan asked.

"Oh, shit," Lance said. "This guy is sick."

Two hours later they'd wrapped up to leave the scene.

It was past midnight.

"I'm not sure what we have, except we can hold the asshole on stalking or domestic violence for at least a couple of days to find out what forensics uncovers," Lance said.

The forensic team was busy, collecting the photographs, bagging his electronic equipment in plastic bags, various other items of interest.

"Man, look at all of these burner phones," Ryan said as he put everything in the drawer in another plastic bag.

"The computer guys are going to be in heaven, uncovering what Thomas has on his hard drive," Lance said.

"It's going to take a while to uncover the codes and passwords, but I think we've hit the gold mine with that," Reid replied. "I think what we discover on the computer is going to do Eric Thomas in."

Lance's cell phone rang. "Damn, can't I have thirty minutes without the phone? What?"

"Harris, it's Rosen. Some big-shot attorney is here demanding that Thomas be released."

"Isn't going to happen. You tell him we have DNA that needs to be processed and a room full of pictures of women, at least over five hundred, and until we determine what that is about, he can sit his ass in jail."

"You want me to start the processing tonight?"

"We'll see what the judge says tomorrow. I don't have to do shit until his arraignment. I won't be back until tomorrow after the funeral of Melissa Sikes, so there's no getting out until I get there, probably around noon."

"What if the attorney demands to talk to you?"

"Tell him he is welcome to talk to me tomorrow afternoon at the station."

"Sure thing."

"Ryan, I need to make a call." He stepped outside, hitting Claire's cell number.

Claire answered after the second ring.

"Hello," Claire said softly. She sounded so fragile. Lance was worried.

"Claire, are you feeling okay? I know it's not a good time, but I just wanted you to know I'm thinking of you and I'll see you tomorrow. Stay safe. You call me immediately if you need anything."

Claire started to ask about the latest, but decided she couldn't take anymore right now.

"Lance, you calling me means so much. I'm pulling in all of my resources, praying, slowly finding my strength." She paused to take a breath. "I will call you if I need you. I'm getting ready to lay down."

"You are special, Claire. I'm here for you."

"I'm here for you. Goodnight."

"Take care." Lance hung up the phone and stared ahead. Lance knew when this was all behind them, he was getting back with Claire and hoped she felt the same. He remembered the family motto, 'Never give up.'

CHAPTER TWENTY-ONE

It was six in the morning when Lance's cell phone rang again.

"Harris."

"Lance, I just heard from Haley in forensics," Spencer said. "He thinks he may have a DNA link between Thomas and a brutal rape last year during the Mavericks basketball playoff games. I remember working the case."

"I remember it, too. She came in; Delphina I think was her name. We did a lineup, but no such luck. I think Davis was keeping up with the case. Can you call him? Let's get this rolling. I'm going to the funeral this morning and then meeting Thomas' attorney later. That son-of-a-bitch isn't going anywhere."

"Wonder if she can ID him?"

"Let's pray she does."

Lance dragged himself out of bed and headed for the shower.

Thirty minutes later he was on his way to the Douglas Funeral Home, meeting the other detectives to get in place early and watch.

Claire was up early, trying to get herself together and get ready for Melissa's funeral. It was at ten, and Vanessa was doing the early show for her. She started gathering up her purse and things she was taking with her this morning when her cell phone rang. She picked it up off of the nightstand and saw it was Lance. She answered.

"Claire, I wanted to check on you. I'm on my way to the funeral home now, and I'll be looking for you when you get there," Lance said. "Are you doing okay? As good as can be in this horrible situation?"

Softly, Claire replied, "I'm doing the best I can." She couldn't say anything more, or she knew she would start crying.

"Look for me when you get there, and I'll be looking for you. Take care and be safe. I'll see you in a little while."

"Thanks, Lance, see you in an hour," she said as she slowly hung up the phone and laid it back on the table. It meant so much to Claire that he called.

She dragged herself into the bathroom. Her dogs, Copper and Ginger, came in and licked her leg, a sign they wanted to go out. They had been at her neighbor's house all day. They babysat the puppies for her sometimes. Chandler had been kind to go get them from her neighbor last night before he left.

"Melissa, no. Please God, no," and Claire fell to her knees in the shower.

Fifteen minutes later she was drying off with a renewed sense to find out what happened to her friend and determined to stop the killer.

Dressed in a black dress and heels, Claire grabbed her briefcase, keys, let the dogs inside and headed out to her Hummer. Claire had to prepare herself, mentally and emotionally, because she'd be doing the story on Melissa's funeral for the five, six and ten pm newscasts. She was planning to meet her co-workers, Becky, Valerie and Hillary at the Starbucks down the street from the Douglas Funeral Home, located on the outskirts of Highland Park. She'd have to pass it before she arrived at the coffee shop.

She spotted Lance's truck at the front of the funeral home.

When she reached Starbucks, her co-workers were standing out front waiting for her.

"Let's get some coffee. I just saw Detectives Harris and Sanchez at the funeral home. I'm sure they are getting set up," Claire said. Lance and Reid met Detectives Davis and Ryan at the funeral home, along with some undercover police detectives.

"I want everyone positioned at the funeral home to observe all the action, like who comes in, then be ready to move to the gravesite," Lance said. "We already have officers there, so we'll join them. Do not stick out. Everyone have your earwig in place so you can communicate with our police offsite. They're in a white van behind the funeral home grounds on standby if we need them. Ready?"

"Yes sir," the detectives replied.

"Let's move."

Melissa's extended family members were starting to arrive: aunts, uncles, cousins. The whole scene was heart-wrenching. Her parents had been inside since six that morning.

Tables were set up throughout, with photos and mementos with photographs of Melissa throughout her life, from baby pictures, family vacations, her years of playing softball in high school and pictures of her at college with her sorority sisters, her boyfriend and last of all, a large photograph of Melissa and Claire in front of the Channel Two television studio.

Her close friends, cousins, her brother and sister were all standing in a circle, holding each other up.

Lance placed himself in the corner, where he could see who greeted her parents and brother, Jim, as well as her sister, Julie.

For more than an hour, people of all ages greeted her family, then were quickly escorted into the chapel.

So far, nothing had alarmed Lance. He remembered that this funeral home was one of the largest in the city, and housed several chapels of different sizes. The one his family had been in when his aunt recently died was much smaller. This room looked to be their largest one. There was a podium in the front and a large screen hanging open behind it.

Moments later, Claire and her co-workers entered the chapel. Julie began to cry when she saw Claire, and the girl ran to her, throwing her arms around her.

The howling from Melissa's sister was devastating and Lance noticed tears running down Claire's cheeks, as well as the other ladies. They were all enclosed in a circle around each other.

"Claire, I want Melissa back," Julie cried as she held on to her. "I'm going to do what Melissa was going to do. I'm going to get a journalism degree and became a great journalist, just like Melissa." She slumped in Claire's arms, obviously emotionally depleted.

"She was so proud of you, Julie," Claire said, sniffling. "I will be there with you all along the way."

Patsy, Melissa's mother, also joined the group of women as she tried to help Julie calm down. The whole place went completely quiet as everyone watched.

"Look around at everyone watching, and see if anyone is suspicious," Lance whispered into the microphone that was clipped on his tie, but out of view. He noticed that Melissa's father, John Wilkes, could only look on, appearing unable to move.

Just as the women began to break up and make their way toward the chapel, several of the young ushers came to the ladies to take their elbows and help them walk. Julie fell into the arms of one young man who had to practically carry her down the aisle to where Melissa's family would be seated. He stayed with her until Jim appeared.

Ten minutes later, the music began. "Amazing Grace" filled the chapel hall as a female soloist belted out the words.

Melissa's parents walked down the aisle as everyone stood, heads bowed, many fighting back tears.

Pastor Tim Marshall came up to the podium. Behind him, they began flashing a video montage of Melissa's life.

Lance had moved again, to a secret place where he could watch. He ventured a quick glance at Claire, who at that exact moment happened to look up and see him.

She looked so sad. Lance did something he'd never done before; he blew her an imaginary kiss.

She returned it and looked back at the pastor.

That was it for Lance. He was going to do everything he could to win her back. Claire—she was in his heart. He said a quick prayer, and it was back to what was expected of him.

Catch this demon killer.

"Sanchez?" Lance whispered, looking down so no one would catch him and think he was talking to himself.

His partner's answer was quick. "There must be at least fifty photographers, watching all of them. Greg is here and so is Chandler. That asshole seems nervous, looking everywhere. I'm keeping an eye on him."

"Everyone, be ready, three minutes and they'll be coming out." Lance turned back around and then the video montage had stopped at a recent photograph of Melissa with her family at a lake.

What a beautiful family.

Pastor Marshall began his eulogy to a totally silent room. He spoke of Melissa and about all of the great achievements she had accomplished in her short life. It was at that moment the sounds of sniffles and crying began to fill the background of the church. He spoke of Melissa and her family and how they had played an important role in the building and growth of the church. He then ended Melissa's eulogy with a prayer.

Then, the family stood and the young lady who sang earlier grabbed the microphone and stood to the side. The Wilkes walked up to the stage. The pastor handed Mr. Wilkes the microphone.

"We thank you with all of our hearts for your prayers, cards, calls and notes. We're going to close our service with Melissa's favorite song, 'Amazing Love,'" He choked up, handing the microphone back.

The singer started singing "Amazing Love," first, without any music in the background, and then with a man softly playing his guitar.

Everyone stood, and it was as if no one could move. Then the exit line moved slowly.

Lance had never seen anything like it. He left to go to his next position. The other detectives would remain in place until the chapel cleared, as ordered.

As the beautiful song continued, Melissa's mother sobbed, and her husband put his arm around her shoulders to lead her down the aisle. There were funeral escorts waiting to take the family to the waiting limo outside.

Claire and her co-workers, along with a few other members of the media filed out as it was their turn amongst the crowd. They were met by the lights and flashes of photographers' cameras and video cameras.

That was when Claire heard the first shout.

"Ms. McKenzie, do you have any comment on Eric Thomas being arrested for assaulting you? He's now a suspect in the Smiley Face murders!" Claire was stunned and stopped in her tracks. She took a quick breath to get herself together. "I have no comment. How *dare* you ask me anything here at the funeral of a fellow co-worker and friend. Show some respect."

Her co-workers joined arms with her in a show of camaraderie at the bottom of the stairs. She noticed Chandler had his camera fixed on her. Even Greg was shaking his head when he must've noticed, too. *What a total jerk.*

The burial was closed to anyone but close family and invited friends. Claire didn't blame Melissa's family for doing that. Claire had decided not to go to the burial.

She took a second to call Lance on his cell.

"Harris."

"You know it's me. Do you have anything new?"

"We're holding Thomas on a sexual assault charge at this time."

"I'm out of it. No charges from me. I can't be a part of this. Find the killing bastard." She hung up, her face in a tight mad frown. She was furious with Lance and the police.

By early afternoon, the media was all over Eric and Claire's incident. They swarmed, trying to find out how Eric came to be at Claire's and how he suddenly became a suspect in the murders.

She was lonely and wanted to see Lance.

They had Valerie doing the Eric Smiley Face Killer investigation since it was now a conflict of interest for Claire to do it.

She had to get ready for her live shot, but first things first—news conference on the front steps at KABC for the other media.

They had been calling, stopping by the station, and in a sense, demanding Claire give them a statement.

Michael Chase, that jerk reporter from Channel Nine had a smarmy smile on his face when Claire took the microphone for questions. She was going to make it short and sweet.

CHAPTER TWENTY-TWO

Lance headed back to his office, takeout bag in hand. He needed to work on a timeline for Jessica and Melissa. His cell blared, yanking him away from his plan.

"Harris."

"I may have something. We got a fingerprint on the knife we found in Melissa's apartment. It's going through the AFIS system now, so far no luck, but I'm just going to let it roll," Spencer said. "I scraped what I could from her fingernails, and we could have DNA, some kind of damn break. She put up quite a fight, and I'll tell you right now, whoever this creep is, he has bruises to show for it."

"Spencer, let me know as soon as the DNA results are in." Reid popped in as soon as Lance hit the end button.

"Word is the Mayor is here and wants to know what the problem is," his partner said.

"Keep him away from me. I might lose it," Lance replied as he walked into his office. He started going through paperwork left on his desk and turned on his computer. He looked up and saw Mayor Hamilton enter his office in a huff.

"Chief Deputy Detective Harris, I need to know what is going on," Hamilton said loudly.

"Sir, I can't share any information because we are still conducting the investigation and we don't have a conclusion yet," Harris said sternly.

"What, you have nothing?" Hamilton said.

"We are investigating several developments, and we don't want any information to be released at this time."

"Are you implying that I would release important information? You have twenty-four hours to make an arrest, or your job could be in jeopardy," Hamilton yelled as he stormed out of the office.

Shaking his head, Harris sat down and pulled up a file on his computer. Back to work to catch this bastard.

Claire planned on going on air live at five with her story first, Melissa's funeral, followed by Valerie's story on the latest on the Smiley Face murder, and a more in depth look at Eric Thomas being investigated as a suspect. She ended her segment with a few closing remarks about his attack on Claire.

She wasn't happy about the editorial decision that she should talk about that bastard Eric and do an informal news conference, but she did. They'd argued back and forth until finally the News Director told Claire she was too emotionally distraught with all that'd happened to her to make a decision.

Back live at six, Claire led with Melissa's funeral, and Valerie went with the story on Eric and her again, the latest on finding Melissa's murderer and how they were investigating how he may be linked to the Smiley Face Killer, although police hadn't said publicly that Melissa's killer was the Smiley Face Killer.

Claire was exhausted, and her boss told her to go home, even though it was barely seven. It was almost summer, and the sun was still out. She didn't argue with the News Director, and when she got home, she planned on a refreshing run at the park across the street from her house. As she got ready for her run, she was thinking about Lance. He had her heart, and she knew she had to do something about it. No more waiting. Her face and expressions slowly changed.

She was going for a run. At first, she was exhilarated. Sweat beaded her brows and slid down her spine. She held on to her exhilaration, feeling much better than she did before. The muscles in her legs responded great to the run so far.

About a half a mile in, Claire had a strange sensation that someone was watching her. She halted and planted her palms on her knees. She'd been at a brisk clip instead of the jog she'd intended. Pushing hard made her lungs burn.

Claire glanced around, noticing other runners on the opposite side of the path, and some even jog past her. She couldn't shake the sensation. Her inside alarms were going off, telling her to be alert and to be careful.

Maybe I should just go home.

She spotted her neighbor, Ralph Pinkston, working in his yard. He lived a couple of houses from her. She should stop and say hello and thank him and his family for always helping her with the dogs. She needed normal people in her life, not all the chaos that had been going on. Melissa's funeral, plus all the drama at the station, had her in a mess, and her tummy was churning. Claire needed to get a grip on everything, including Lance. She couldn't stop obsessing about him. *Where is he? Does Lance care for me?*

"Hey Claire, I've been watching you on the news. Man, if I'd known that guy tried to hit on you at your own house, I would've killed him myself."

Claire's gaze raked Ralph's six-foot-three, former college-football player frame. Now married with three young children. Nice guy, and it was great to have their family in her neighborhood.

"It's been unbelievable. I bit him on the shoulder, and ran like hell upstairs to call 911."

Ralph was laughing so hard he nearly dropped his trimmer.

"Only you would think to bite a guy, not kick him."

"Oh, no, I kicked him too, right in the balls."

Ralph laughed harder. "Claire, only you. Hey, I'm serious, you call me anytime. Our family is here for you. We loved your grandmother when she lived there, and we are so glad you're there now."

Emotion jumped up for Claire. For a moment Claire thought she was going to cry. Her family had called and left messages, and when Claire had called back, she told them everything that had happened. She'd worshipped her grand-mother, who had passed away a couple of years ago, leaving a huge void in Claire's life. Nina—that's what she called her—she had always been there for her growing up, and Claire would never forget it.

"Ralph, if you ever hear a scream, head my way. I appreciate the offer, and I'll call you if I need anything," Claire patted him on the back.

"I mean it. There're lots of weirdoes out there. Hey, did you hear some guy, maybe in his thirties, rented Ms. Grayson's house down the street? Don't know much else about him. Strange that a young guy would move into a neighborhood full of old folks or families with kids. I don't mean anything about you—your grandmother left you the house and it has special memories. You'll find a man, settle here with all of us, and have lots of kids."

"I haven't heard about him moving in until now, but I'll follow up and see what I can find out. Can't help it, the reporter in me," Claire smiled and waved again as she started to trot across the street to her house.

"Let me know," Ralph called back to her.

A young man in his thirties. That is odd around here. Maybe I need to let Lance know.

Claire unlocked her new front door that her News Direc-tor, thankfully, had taken care of and had gotten it replaced from the damage the other day.

Once she was inside she hit her office, on her computer, and did needed research on the Internet. Thirty minutes later, the distraction wasn't what she'd hoped.

What would Nina do about feeling so sad? Cook!

Claire laughed for the first time in a long time. *Cook! My dear grandmother from Mobile, Alabama would be in the kitchen.* Thinking about Lance and wondering where he was, she grabbed her purse and went to the farmers market and fish market down on Oak Lawn. Claire should cook a good, healthy dinner with salad, vegetables and shrimp. Some good ole' Shrimp Creole with rice

Lance met with the FBI, his friend, Special Agent Jake Russell, to get set up with the latest on what FBI profiler Whitney had come up with. They had a quick catch up and then left. Lance then called the Chief in to stroke his ego. He felt as if he knew the killer.

The killer must strike again. He can't help himself.

Chandler hit the bars looking for his next victim. Chandler selected the bar where all the media-types hang out and spied Valerie. It was after the six o'clock newscast. She wasn't expected back until the late news.

Chandler walked up behind Valerie as she stood at the bar drinking a glass of wine and nuzzled a kiss on her cheek.

Valerie abruptly turned around and slightly screamed, "Chandler, what are you doing? You scared me silly."

Jeremy Chandler displayed the smile he knew all of the women liked. Valerie was perfect. She didn't have many friends at the station because she kept to herself and was determined to beat everyone with the latest news story scoop no matter what.

They talked about work and the latest stories both of them were working on. Jeremy never brought up Claire's name because he knew Valerie was jealous of how the public liked and enjoyed Claire as a reporter and anchor.

Thirty minutes later Valerie left with her new admirer.

Lance watched the six newscast in his office. There was no sign of Claire. Did that mean she wasn't going to be on at ten either?

He stood and stretched, then looked out the window of his office. Lance was done for the day. He didn't belong at work anymore. He grabbed his jacket off the hanger.

It had been a long, hard day, and he needed Claire.

CHAPTER TWENTY-THREE

Claire turned on Keith Urban and did a little twirl as she let her dogs, Copper and Ginger, out the backdoor and the screen door swung shut. She mirrored Keith's voice in "Without You."

She left the door open for fresh air and swayed to the music on her way into the kitchen. Claire pulled out a bottle of champagne from the fridge and grabbed the wine opener. She kept on dancing around the kitchen as she got together cooking supplies and pans. "Got to have champagne when you're cooking Shrimp Creole."

She'd banished the idea of stress and depression from her mind—at least for the evening. She had to keep going. Claire wouldn't forget, but she could keep herself together, and prayed the killer was found, and her friend—as well as Jessica and Melissa—could both truly be at rest.

Dancing, singing and cooking would make her feel better. Claire thought about Lance and wondered where he was. She knew she always wanted to cook her grandmother's favorite recipe for him. Claire knew Lance would love it.

The doorbell rang. It was after eight pm, and the sun was beginning its descent. Who could be at the door?

She hesitated; her heart thundered. A shudder racked her frame, and fear took a bite out of Claire.

No. She couldn't be afraid in her own house.

Claire peered out the peephole in the front door. Her heart skipped.

Lance was standing there with red and white wine bottles and a dozen red roses.

Everyone had been calling, checking on her, but she'd stopped answering the phone. Had he called?

He's here.

Claire opened the door.

"I need you, Claire."

Her tears blurred her vision even more and she whimpered.

He put the wine bottles on the entrance hall table and took her into his arms.

"It's okay." Claire was overcome with tears of happiness and sadness over the loss of her friend and co-worker, Melissa, and now the happiness of being in the arms of Lance. He was holding her.

"I have dinner going. You dropped by at the right time. I need to get back to it so it doesn't burn."

Lance followed closely, sliding his arms around her as she stepped up to the stove to stir her Shrimp Creole. He leaned in to kiss her neck, inhaling her perfume, and it turned him on.

"I need you," Lance whispered as she slowly turned around and pushed up tip-toed for a kiss.

It went on forever, a kiss of want, need and *now*.

"Come with me," Claire turned the stove on low and took Lance's hand. Urgency built inside her and she could barely keep it calm as they headed to her bedroom. He remembered, kisses and touches carried them to her king bed. Claire stared at his muscular body and chest.

Then his hands were on her. His hands explored her cheeks and neck, traveling down. He leaned over and kissed her again.

Claire didn't fight him. She wanted this. Wanted him. She leaned in to him and she can feel the force of his body, and all of the emotions inside of her hit.

He sat on the edge of the bed and drew her closer. Lance plastered kisses all over her.

Claire buried her hands in his dark hair and tossed her head back, gasping.

They melted into the bed, with her against his chest. Her heart sped up, threatening to exit her chest.

Lance gazed down into the most beautiful face in the world.

He loved her.

Lance wanted her as much as she needed him.

An hour later, Claire pushed in to Lance's larger body and positioned her smaller feminine form into him. There was nothing more to say. He was where he belonged. He'd never leave again. Lance settled in beside her and pulled her closer, as close as he could get her. Claire nestled her head on his chest, and sighed.

A smile played at his mouth, and Lance echoed her contentment. His eyes were heavy, so he gave in to the desire to close them. Drifting off to sleep was next, but it was perfect, just like Claire.

CHAPTER TWENTY-FOUR

They were still in bed when Claire's phone rang, jarring her awake. Something warm and solid was against her body.

Lance.

The evening rushed back, and she smiled as she reached for the screaming cell. He was awake, too. Watching her with a smirk on his delicious mouth. She was sorry her call had woken him, but her insides wobbled from the look on his face.

"Hello?" she asked. It was Hillary, from work. "No, she's sorry she missed the ten pm newscast. She fell asleep." Claire winked at Lance, and he grinned.

Hillary explained that they didn't have a chance to call before the news because they'd been scrambling to figure out what to do. Valerie hadn't shown up.

"That's not like her at all."

Although Claire didn't think much of Valerie, she respected her work ethic.

The fellow reporter would never miss a story or newscast.

"I'm worried too. Let me know if you hear anything." Claire frowned as she set her phone down.

"Is something wrong?"

She nodded. "Maybe. Valerie didn't come back for the ten newscast."

"Knowing her, she snagged another poor soul, or maybe

she had too much to drink and passed out."

"Maybe you're right. Hillary said they were going to call the police though," she said.

"Let's give it a couple of hours before we get concerned. Now where was I?"

Oh yeah...

"I'll be right back. I need to put the Shrimp Creole in the refrigerator."

Moments later Claire returned.

Lance rubbed Claire's back and urged her to him.

Lance's cell phone rang. His arms were wrapped around Claire, but he untangled to answer. He frowned when he noticed the time. It was after two in the morning.

"What's up?" Lance asked the dispatcher.

"We got a call from Channel Two earlier. Valerie Newton didn't show up for work and they decided to go by her apartment. Some of her co-workers got inside her apartment, and there was no sign she'd been home today. They wanted to report her missing because of the Smiley Face Killer. Thought you would want to know."

"Who reported her missing?"

"Her News Director, Tim Carlson and a Channel Two photographer, Jeremy Chandler."

"Call me if anything comes up. I'll be there by six."

At five in the morning, he got another call. It was Reid.

"Harris."

"I just got in, and there was a call from a guy who's been out of town, but he was jogging early in the morning on the day Jessica's body was found in the park. He just got back into town last night, and his friends were telling him about Jessica. He said he thinks he saw the guy and wants to talk to us. Said he would be here at eight."

"I'm on my way."

He leaned over. Claire was awake and staring up at him.

Oh, what a beautiful sight.

Lance kissed her. She smiled from her pillow.

They got up moving, and he hit the shower. Lance liked the feeling of waking up next to her. Being in her bed, holding her, then starting their collective days.

He gave his thanks when she handed him a steaming cup of coffee in her bright, welcoming kitchen. "What's going on?" Claire asked.

"I don't know, but be careful."

"I'm worried about Valerie." Claire trembled and looked as if she was holding back tears.

"I'll do everything I can."

"I'm scared," Claire said. She was still in a robe. She'd let him get ready first.

"Go finish getting ready. If you want, I can drop you off at the station."

"I'll need my car today, and you have a long day ahead too, but thanks," Claire said.

Lance waited for her, despite the fact he *should* hurry in to the police station. He didn't want to part from Claire until he had to. He made some calls from the kitchen, but she hadn't come back down yet. He should check on her.

When he made it into her bedroom, she'd just finished applying her lipstick. His gaze raked her black dress and the slit up the side. Lance had to swallow hard. They looked at each other in the mirror before she turned to him.

He tugged her close, couldn't help it. Of its own accord, his hand ran from her thigh, along her bare skin up her hip.

Lance groaned.

Claire leaned back and looked at him. A dare. Their lips met and they were again swept away in passion, and in each other.

Even though he didn't want to let her go, Lance had to release her. He knew he loved her.

Claire stood and fixed her dress.

Lance took her in his arms one more time. He had to kiss the look off her face.

Claire is trying not to cry. "Why is this happening?"

"I don't know, but I'll stop it."

"Valerie can't be gone. Find her, Lance."

"You be safe. Do *not* go anywhere by yourself. I want all of you in groups."

"I'll be careful." Claire grabbed her makeup bag, briefcase and some Kleenex. "Wait just a minute for me, if you don't mind." She slipped into the bathroom.

Lance gazed out the bedroom window.

Silently, she joined him. The scent of her perfume swirled around, making him want her again, but they didn't have time. He slid his arm around her, pinning her to his side. He'd keep her here, locked away all day if he could. So he wouldn't have to worry about her.

"You be safe and call me. I don't care if you think it's nothing important, you call," he said.

Claire threw Lance a key when they hit the foyer. "You want to lock up?"

"Sure."

"I know, Lance. I'm scared, but I know you'll get this bastard."

Claire waved okay as she pulled out of the driveway. The garage door automatically closed.

Lance locked up and headed out the front door, checking the dead bolt again.

She threw him one last wave when the Hummer turned onto the street, and he returned it. Wished he'd said something else, like how he felt about her.

Lance couldn't shake this bad feeling he had. It was just past six, so he needed to hold it together and stop being paranoid. Claire would be fine. He'd see her tonight, and he had a long ass day ahead.

When he got in, the news of the bulletin for Valerie Newton already being out greeted him.

Claire arrived at work. There was an ominous atmosphere in the newsroom.

Everyone was scared.

Hillary was working on the morning lineup. They had talked to Valerie's parents, and they had gone to the police department, waiting to interview with a detective.

"We're going with Valerie being missing. Claire, get on it."

Claire didn't know how much more she could take.

CHAPTER TWENTY-FIVE

Money talked, and for Johnny that meant freedom.

The prison guard he'd been paying thousands of dollars to in order to get easy work assignments and perks on death row had certainly paid off again. The escape would cost him one hundred thousand dollars since the doors would have to be opened for him to switch with his brother to walk out a free man. Johnny had a cousin, one he trusted, helping him with the money transfer. He knew he would keep his mouth shut with a little financial incentive.

There was plenty of commotion going on in this prison wing, since it was visitation day for attorneys.

Just what he needed.

Within moments of his brother Clark arriving, he was escorted to a small conference room at the back of the prison unit.

The huge steel doors were open and he was waiting. As soon as Clark attempted to shake Johnny's hand, he plunged the needle in Clark's shoulder.

His eyes went wide and glassy.

"Why?" The whisper was all he got out before he fell to the concrete floor.

Watson quickly undressed his twin, changing into his clothes as the dirty prison guard watched the hallway.

He'd gone to high school with the guard, and money aside, the dude owed him one.

"It's time to leave. I'll tell them at the checkout point down the hall that Johnny Watson's fallen ill and we need emergency medical personnel."

"We'll have six minutes to go down four halls and seven doors to get through the exit. You do not say a word. Just keep moving," the prison guard told Watson.

Watson nodded.

He grabbed his radio. "Officer Porter, I need emergency personnel in room eight immediately. Prisoner Johnny Watson collapsed."

"Yes, sir. Right away."

The prison guard unlocked the door. Medical personnel descended on the room.

"What happened?" one of the paramedics asked.

"I don't know. He just fainted. I'll be right back. I need to escort his attorney out." He shoved Watson through the door and closed it. "Go." The prison guard held on to Johnny.

At the first checkpoint he was waved through because that'd been the officer he'd contacted about getting the emergency personnel to come.

"Keep going." The guard swiped his ID and the next steel door opened.

On and on, they went through the doors.

Coming up to the last door, the prison guard opened it to the parking lot where the prison employees parked.

"Let's go. Now." The guy said as he pushed Watson out the door. "This way to my truck."

Johnny followed. "What are you doing?"

"I'm out of here. I have my money. I don't have any family or wife, so I am out of here to start a new life."

He popped the doors to his truck with his key holder. Phil and Watson jumped in, he started the truck and pulled out of the employee parking lot of the state prison.

Phil grabbed a disposable cell phone and handed it to Watson.

"Here's a cell, where do you want me to drop you? I have to get out of here fast."

"The McDonald's on 14th Street in town. My attorney is there waiting for my call." He dialed the cell phone number.

"Ten minutes."

Phil pulled his truck into the McDonald's parking lot.

"Don't say another word. Just get out. I don't want to know anything."

Johnny got out of the truck and Phil's tires squealed and the dust flew up as he rushed away.

Watson looked around and saw his attorney's Cadillac. He walked slowly towards him, still trying to realize that he was free. He opened the door and slid in.

"I've taken care of everything you asked for. I rented the house down from Claire McKenzie last week. Your keys and rental agreement are in the glove box. There's food and furniture, and I dropped off some of your computer equipment. I had to be careful. The neighbors were getting suspicious."

"Just get the hell to Dallas." Watson closed his eyes to sleep.

Back at Dallas Police headquarters, Lance winced.

It was loud in the homicide division offices as detectives worked on the phone or their computers.

"Reid, I'll be in the interview room with the third jogger. He saw another man, and he has a description."

He walked in. "Good morning, I'm Detective Lance Harris," he said as he shook his hand. "Mr. Martin Taylor, right?"

The man nodded. Taylor was thin, but muscular, and probably in his late fifties.

"Please sit down." Lance gestured to the seat across from the one he took.

"Thank you for seeing me on such short notice. I've been out of town, and when I returned, everyone at work was talking about the Smiley Face Killer."

"Thank you for coming in. Can you tell me what you remember?"

"I was jogging in that area, coming down the hill. I remember seeing two men, one was going the opposite direction. The one I've been thinking about, he was leaning down, like he was tying his shoes. But now that I've had time to think about it, he was hiding something. He didn't appear to have broken a sweat either, and he was covered in a hoodie. I barely got a glance of his face. He stood up for a couple of seconds, turned the opposite direction and took off. I thought it was odd to be wearing a hoodie in this heat. At first I thought, just a weirdo, but now, something doesn't seem right."

"Can you give me a description, Mr. Taylor?"

"I can tell you that he was wearing navy blue sweatpants and a black hoodie jacket. The one time he turned and quickly looked at me he was a white male, and I think with light brown hair," Taylor continued. "I would say he was big and muscular too. Sorry I can't give you any more. I didn't see a mustache."

As Lance took notes, his cell blared. He glanced at the screen. "Sorry, I have to take this. Harris."

"I just talked to Thompson in forensics. When they were clearing and labeling all of the evidence from Melissa's apartment, at the bottom of the box was a crumpled up piece of paper. It said, 'Claire, beware.' I told you before, I think he watched them do the interview with Jessica's friends, then went after Melissa," Reid said.

"I think she was trying to warn Claire, and he shut her up."

"Get it checked for fingerprints," Lance said as anger and

fear raced through his body.

"He must've been in her apartment. Where are you now? You get to KABC and round up all of the women, especially Claire, and no one leaves until I get there and we come up with a game plan. I'm finishing up and will be there ASAP."

He pocketed his cell. "Mr. Taylor, thank you for your time. We will get a bulletin out immediately."

"You catch this bastard," Taylor said as he shook Lance's hand.

Lance returned to his computer and updated the latest suspect description, according to Taylor. He sent it to Dallas Police Communication Officer, Preston Pierce and then grabbed his jacket.

"If any of you need me or Sanchez, we'll be at the KABC studios," he announced to all the cops in the bullpen. He's going for Claire.

CHAPTER TWENTY-SIX

Pierce released a new description of the suspect to all of the news media.

Claire read the latest news release on the suspect's description, but it could be so many men in their late twenties, early thirties. He was tall, six-one to six-three and muscular. He'd been seen wearing a black hoodie jacket pulled up over his head. Maybe brown hair, but unable to be confirmed.

It was hard for her to concentrate, when all she could think about was Valerie.

There was a panic in the air, that only worsened every moment their Co-worker remained unaccounted for.

Sitting at her desk cubicle, Claire heard someone crying down the hall.

Carlson, the KABC News Director, made an announcement over the intercom.

"I'd like for all of the KABC news and production staff to report to the studio. Dallas Police Deputy Chief Detective Lance Harris and Detective Reid Sanchez will be there to bring us up to date on the investigation and what we need to be doing. Please be on time." Carlson choked up at the end, and quickly shut down.

The crying turned into a quiet sobbing. Claire saw Dwight walking that direction, and she prayed he could help.

Lance briefed Reid along with Detectives Ryan and Davis, before they joined all the station's staff.

"I want each of you in separate offices or conference rooms to interview anyone who comes forward, but particularly, those who were at the nightclub that night between newscasts and saw Valerie there, and if they saw her leave with anyone," Lance said.

Carlson, the News Director, greeted them, along with the station manager.

"Detective Harris, if you and your men would follow me, we have everyone in the studio waiting."

No one spoke as they continued down the hallway. Carlson opened a steel door, and immediately the studio cameras and anchor desk were visible.

Chairs had been set up, but the employees were positioned all over the place.

Lance spotted Claire and her friends sitting in chairs at the front. Lance felt the pull in his gut, the need, the want, for Claire. To protect his special lady.

The detectives were escorted to a podium that sported a microphone. The faces of the news reporters, cameramen, engineers, told the story. "Fear."

There was no denying tension and fear in the studio.

Lance had a distinct, stern expression that told everyone he meant business, serious business. Lance had been surveying the studio, checking out the different expressions. He could barely see the faces of the people at the very back. Were they trying to hide something?

"Ladies and gentlemen, I have with me, Dallas Police Deputy Chief Homicide Detective Harris and Homicide Detective Sanchez, and Detectives Ryan and Davis." Carlson stepped back from the microphone.

"Good afternoon. We're doing everything we can to find Valerie Newton. We have three rooms available to use for interviews. If you worked with her in the last couple of days, if you were with her last night before she left, or if you were at the nightclub last night, please make yourself available to us. You may have information useful in helping us find her. Please, if you have additional information about Melissa, please share that with us as well. Go in groups tonight. Do not go anywhere alone. It would be best for the next couple of days, for you to not stay alone. If you do, please make sure your doors are all locked and don't open the door until you know exactly who's there. Any questions?"

A hand shot up.

Lance pointed. "In the back."

"Why can't the Dallas police arrest the 'Smiley Face Killer?'" someone yelled, and some of his photographer friends high-fived him.

It was everything Lance could do to hold it together, especially when he realized it was that jerk, Jeremy Chandler.

Claire closed her eyes and leaned over to Hillary. "Why does Chandler have to be such an asshole?"

"We can't disclose any information at this time, but I can assure you he will be caught. Thank you for your time. If you could please join us in the adjoining rooms, we'd be glad to talk to you," Lance said.

As the group dispersed, several people lined up in front of the rooms the detectives had already set up inside. One by one, KABC employees entered.

Lance encountered Claire and Hillary as he was headed to join Reid in one of the rooms.

Claire touched his arm, and he reached for her hand.

"Claire, you and Hillary be careful. This guy knows you somehow, I am convinced. He knows you personally." Claire's gorgeous blue eyes widened. Lance hated to frighten her, but he had to be real with her. She had to be safe. He would have to tell her about the note, see if she'd forgotten to tell him something, but he was dreading it.

"Can we talk to you down the hall?" Hillary asked.

"Certainly." He steered the ladies in the opposite direction of the interview rooms.

Hillary led them to her office and quietly closed the door.

Both ladies started crying and talking at the same time, and Lance pulled them both into his arms.

"I'm sorry, Lance," Claire whispered.

"I am always here for you, and your friends. I need to know everything about last night."

The women pulled back and wiped their faces with Kleenex.

"Detective," Hillary said.

"Lance."

She nodded. Hillary flipped her long, blonde hair to her back and looked up at Lance with small tears shining in her green eyes.

"Lance, when Valerie left the studio last night after the six newscast, she was worked up over something."

Claire stood back and listened. She hadn't heard this information before.

"This is just my woman's intuition coming out, but I felt like it was over a guy, and not about everything that had happened the last couple of days. Valerie was being somewhat snippy and rude to everyone, more than usual, and she was constantly trying to call someone on her cell phone."

"Do you know who she's dating?" Lance asked.

"Not that I know of. Claire?" Hillary looked at Claire.

"I don't know. We were friends, but not best friends."

"It wasn't unusual for her to leave between shows. It would bother me sometimes, but she always came back on time, and never missed her slot on the ten newscast. This time when she walked out the backdoor of the studio I called out to her and she ignored me and slammed the door. I couldn't believe she was leaving, disappearing on a night like last night, after everything that had happened," she paused, and looked as if she'd taken a deep breath. "I tried to call her cell, and she ignored me. She's never done that before. When she didn't return here last night, I kept calling her, up until the opening of the newscast. I decided to call the police, and also called the News Director and our general manager."

"Thank you for doing that Hillary. I need to get back to the station, but call if you need anything. Claire, I'll talk to you later on." He pulled her into a goodbye hug and wanted to kiss her, but thought better of it. Lance couldn't resist a touch to her cheek, though, then he made himself go.

He met with his detectives and a group of female KABC employees. There were lots of hugs, laughter, and the passing around of business cards.

"I hope some investigative work got done in there," Lance said to Reid.

"Oh, yeah."

He shook his head. "Guys and pretty girls. Well, everyone better be ready to give me an update on our way back to the station."

Before they could leave, he needed to see the News Director.

"Carlson, thank you." He put his hand out for a shake.

"Please, you tell me what to do and what you need and it is done. I'm about to lose it. First Melissa, then Valerie," the older man's brown eyes went misty and his voice shook. "Whatever you need, Detective Harris, we will do it."

"Remember what I said today. I'll call you if I need anything or if something comes up. You guys have been straight forward, and I appreciate it. Make sure your female reporters go everywhere in groups, never alone, even out covering a story. I would send extra detail with them."

"Will do. Good luck and catch that son-of-a-bitch. Minutes

ago I received word of a protest scheduled for tomorrow over the lack of an arrest by the police—just FYI."

"Thanks."

Lance hollered at his detectives to meet him outside. He was ready to go.

"Who wants to go first?"

The police remained stationed at Valerie's apartment, and she hadn't shown up.

Her parents, police, and co-workers had no clue where she was.

Fear was racing through the Dallas community, and the story was beginning to go national as Fox News, CNN, and other national media arrived in town to cover the story.

CHAPTER TWENTY-SEVEN

Watson's attorney dropped him in the back of the home he'd rented, two doors down from Claire.

Watson handed him an envelope.

"Never contact me again. If you do, I'll have you killed."

The stunned look on his attorney's face said it all. The man began to shake, then he pushed Johnny backwards and ran outside, jumped in his car and pulled out of the driveway.

He fell back, threw his arm against the floor and was able to find his balance and lift himself up.

"You stupid bastard!" He shook his fist.

Watson regained his composure, looked around and hoped his neighbors didn't see anything. He dashed into the house.

Watson stopped in the kitchen to catch his breath. His heart was beating out of control. He paused for a moment, glanced in to the family room and noticed boxes full of computers, cameras and his telescope equipment.

He grabbed his telescope and raced up the stairs, two at a time, to his bedroom. He threw open the door and focused on his balcony. Johnny fished for his keys and unlocked the balcony door, but he took care to make sure no one noticed him. His telescope anchor was there, his stupid attorney must've set it up for him. Cautiously, he walked over and attached the telescope.

He adjusted his telescope vision towards Claire's house. He could clearly see into her bedroom, and did a quick view of other rooms in her home that were visible through open curtains.

His telescope picked up a strange man walking around her house, peering in to different windows.

He looked familiar to Watson. "I know him. Is that Jeremy?"

It was around four in the afternoon when Lance called Claire on her cell. "Any news on Valerie?"

"No."

"How late are you working tonight?"

"Through the six o'clock newscast, then I'll edit a story for ten. I should be finished by seven-thirty. I'll check in with the police before the late news. They may have someone else go live, since they're worried I'm exhausted. I really am. I'm scared, too." She muffled her mouth, afraid she was going to start crying. All Claire had done was cry, then enter her 'no emotion mode' so she could make it through the day and survive.

"Can I come over?"

"Yes. You told me last night you needed me, Lance. Tonight, I need you."

"Call me before you leave the station and leave me a message."

They hung up without saying goodbye.

Later, Claire headed home. There was nothing more she could do. She was physically exhausted and emotionally spent.

Her mom and other relatives had been calling, but she couldn't deal with that tonight. She'd return calls in the morning. Pulling in her driveway made all the security lights spring to life.

She parked the Hummer in her garage and closed the door. Her movement was like a sloth. It took all her strength to drag her briefcase and her bags to the back door. When Claire slid inside, she made sure to deadbolt the door. She set her stuff down and went to check the front door. "Locked. Good."

Claire called Lance and left him a message that she was home.

One glass of chardonnay, and an hour later after watching the news, Claire slowly made her way up the stairs to her bedroom. Lance hadn't called yet, so she made sure her phone didn't need to be charged. She stopped her thoughts when her eyes landed on her bed, and Claire smiled.

Then, looking in the bathroom mirror startled her back to reality. She was tired. She looked it, too. Much too much for a news reporter. She said a quick prayer that Lance and the police would find Valerie alive and well. And soon.

She took her makeup off, brushed her teeth, threw on a nightgown and she headed to bed. She wished Ginger and Copper were here, but she had set it up earlier in the day with her neighbor again, Ralph, for him to come over and take Ginger and Copper to his house so they could play with their family dog for the next couple of days. He knew what was going on with the Smiley Face Killer and her crazy work schedule.

He and his wife were awesome neighbors.

Claire hadn't known what was ahead and didn't want to put them at the vet for several days.

She grabbed a pillow and prayed Lance and his fellow detectives would be safe. She also prayed Lance would return to her tonight. "I love you, Lance," Claire whispered as she closed her eyes.

An hour later, her cell phone rang, jarring her awake. She'd gotten her wish.

Lance. "I'm outside your door," he said quietly. "I'm on my way." Claire raced down the stairs, looked out the peephole and saw him. *I'm safe,* ran through her mind, over and over. Claire smiled. She opened the door and fell into his arms.

CHAPTER TWENTY-EIGHT

Chandler watched Claire through the glass window of the photographers' office as she walked through the newsroom. It was super early, just past five in the morning and they were all working overtime. Chandler was not happy with Claire.

She hadn't been paying any attention to him. His life was spinning out of control. Maybe he needed to get his prescription refilled and take some medicine before he took his anguish out on Claire. He had to maintain his control. He couldn't let her know he was losing it.

After saying goodbye to Lance out front, Claire ran into the station, dropped her purse and briefcase on her desk and headed to Olivia Taylor's office, the Morning Producer.

Olivia obviously didn't see Claire because she was so intensely caught up typing on her computer, probably putting together the morning show lineup.

"Olivia, I have a question for you."

She jerked her head in Claire's direction. "Oh, my goodness, Claire, you scared me to death."

"Sorry about that. Two things. Anything new on Valerie? Also, I was wondering if you had time for me to do a short live shot, updating the fact the police met with a third jogger and he gave his description of who they believe may be the suspect."

"Nothing on Valerie. And things have changed. Her parents are at the police station now waiting to meet with detectives, so we're leading with Valerie not coming in to work, and that she may be missing." Olivia took a breath. "Yes, on the second part, how long do you need on your story, one minute, or a minute thirty?"

"Yeah, around a minute thirty. I'll give an update as well, and I'll keep calling Val."

"Lead story. Val first, and then update on Jessica and the jogger's description," Olivia nodded her attention back to the computer.

Game on. Claire made a fist. She was going to conquer the day.

Watson couldn't wait. He broke into Claire's house.

He was in her closet, in search of lingerie to feed his fetish. He had the whole day to go through her bedroom, her drawers, her personal items. Then he would get Claire and make her believe that he was innocent, then she would have to help him get free.

He'd lucked out, seeing Claire leave so early this morning. Whoever the Smiley Face Killer was, he was a clever bastard. Watson still harbored the feeling that he knew who it was. Seeing Claire walk out with that bastard Harris that morning, and watching as she'd gotten in the car with him had nearly sent him over the edge to do something dangerous.

For now, it was quiet in the police homicide office. Lance took a sip of the coffee he picked up from Starbucks on the way in before setting it back on his desk.

Control was slipping through his fingertips, and he had a bad feeling. The identity of the Smiley Face Killer was right on the tip of his tongue. His gut said he *knew* him. He was going back over his notes. He was missing something.

But what?

Lance had been told by several of her co-workers and

friends that Valerie was a tough woman and would never leave with someone she didn't know.

The circle was closing. He just hoped he could find Valerie. Save her.

Lance's phone rang. "Harris."

"Sir, the parents of a Valerie Newton are here, and they're very upset because they can't find her. With everything going on they want to file a missing person's report."

"Send them down to my conference room. I need a witness. Who else is in?"

"Sanchez radioed in, and will be here in ten minutes."

"Have them brought to the conference room, and we'll do the interview there. It should only be a few minutes."

"Yes sir."

In another hour, the homicide detectives would be in for the morning meeting.

Lance woke his computer up by jostling the mouse. He hit the Internet to check out news stories. He googled Watson's name. There were at least a thousand links. One caught his eye, the funeral of Gloria Fitzgerald Watson, survivors were twin sons, Clark and Johnny Watson.

Lance froze, his eyes fixed on his computer screen. "Oh, shit."

That call he received on Watson having a twin brother in New York who had disappeared. He called down to dispatch. His gut shouted that all hell was getting ready to break loose.

"Find out more for me about the disappearance of Clark Watson, Johnny Watson's twin brother. Call the state police, too."

He hung up, grabbed his notebook and headed for the conference room with Reid behind him. Standing outside of the door with a patrol officer were Valerie's parents. Harris reached out his hand, shaking Mr. Newton's hand first, just as Reid walked up behind him.

"Good morning, Mr. and Mrs. Newton. I'm Detective Lance Harris, and this is Detective Reid Sanchez. I want you to know we're doing everything we can to find Valerie."

He motioned for the parents to sit down.

Mr. Newton had his arm around his wife and helped her sit in the chair. She was holding a handkerchief to her face as she quietly cried.

"I want to know what's being done," Newton demanded.

"Sir, we interviewed her co-workers yesterday, and today we're interviewing anyone who's been with her in the last week. We also spoke with people who saw her at the nightclub the night she disappeared. We have reports of her leaving with a man, and we have his description. This afternoon, the FBI will meet with us and may join the investigation," Lance said. "Was your daughter seeing anyone? Did she have a steady boyfriend?"

As Valerie's mother quietly cried, her father tilted his head to one side, as if in thought.

"I think there was a young man Valerie was interested in, and she was somewhat discouraged because she felt it was moving slowly, but she never told me his name," her mother answered.

"What about a former boyfriend?" Reid asked.

"There was a man in college, Eugene something. He was two years older than her, but they broke up before she started working at the television station. He's an engineer at AT&T locally. I'll have to look up his information and get back with you."

"Yes, thank you."

"Please know we're doing everything we can to find Valerie. Do you have any other questions?" Lance said.

"No. Just find her. Her high school friends are in the process of putting together a vigil at Warren Park, across from the Dallas Police station for later this afternoon, at five."

"We'll have a police presence there."

Valerie's father had to help his wife up as everyone stood. She grabbed Lance's arm. "Please find my baby," she cried as her husband led her out of the room.

Lance slammed his fist down on the table. "That's it. We find the bastard today. No more!"

CHAPTER TWENTY-NINE

Later that morning, waiting for the FBI to arrive, Lance continued his investigative thought process. Having worked with her on past news stories, Lance knew Valerie was careful. That was what was bothering him. The killer had to be someone in her immediate circle. He could feel it. He hoped to find Valerie before the worst happened. He knew Claire could be in danger, too.

Reid and Davis joined Lance in the police conference room at the end of the offices, waiting for the FBI to arrive.

"You think this is for the best?"

"I don't think we have any other way," Lance said as FBI Special Agent Greg Moore and profiler Curt Horne, well-known in police circles across the country entered the room.

"Good morning." Moore shook Lance's hand.

There was a coffee koozie and cups in the middle of the long table. Moore reached over and poured himself a cup as he sat down.

"I know we're short on time, Horne. Fill us in on what you think so far," Greg said.

"We need to hurry fast and find this son-of-a-bitch."

He looked at Lance. "I think we need to investigate people the newswomen have interviewed in the last two weeks. We need to also look closely at the men working at the television station."

"Let's do it now. Do you have a list of people for the team?"

"Yes."

"Now!" Lance said as Horne made a call.

Throughout the day Claire had been breaking into programming, flashing Valerie's photograph. She was known throughout the community, for her volunteer work with the Susan Komen Breast Cancer Alliance, but especially because of her work as a reporter for KABC. Valerie lost her sister to breast cancer soon after graduating from college.

Claire had a short interview with her Co-worker's parents through a spokesperson, along with her interview with Dallas Police media spokesperson Officer Preston Pierce. Both stories were edited for the five newscast. None of the detectives had granted an interview today. Claire wondered if it was because they had an idea who the killer was, or if they were still searching.

"It's live at five, with Yvette Commerce and Dwight Hall. Tonight, the latest on the search for our Channel Two Crime Reporter, Valerie Newton. Let's go to Claire McKenzie, live at the Dallas Police Department, across the street from Warren Park, where a vigil for Valerie is getting ready to begin. Claire."

The director cut to a full screen picture of Claire

"Thank you, Dwight. The search is ongoing for Channel Two's own Valerie Newton. Dallas Police detectives are quiet today about the investigation. I was able to speak with police spokesperson, Preston Pierce."

As the producer went to her edited story, Claire looked down at her notes, feeling foggy and scared, fear going down her spine.

The story wrapped up.

"We'll have more for you tonight at six, and on the vigil in honor of Valerie, reporting from the downtown Dallas Police Department, Claire McKenzie, Channel Two News."

As she turned away from the camera, a young lady waved to her from behind the live truck.

She was small, with long blonde hair. When Claire approached, she noticed her green eyes.

"Can I help you?"

"Hi, I'm Vickie Monroe," the young woman said, her voice low.

"What can I help you with, Vickie?"

"I was at the nightclub last night when your friend came. I had the feeling she wasn't supposed to be there. She was talking about having to do the ten newscast but needing a drink."

Claire didn't like hearing that, but it was nothing she hadn't heard through the grapevine. Valerie supposedly drank on the clock from time to time. Not acceptable. "Go on."

"I was standing off to the side, just excited to see and be near someone from television. I noticed this guy coming up from behind her, and he whispered in her ear. She turned, started laughing and hugged him, like she knew him."

Claire froze. She was too scared to move. This was the break they'd been looking for. She had to take it slow. This girl was fragile, looked like she might be underage, and not supposed to have been in the nightclub. Claire feared she might take off at any moment. "That's interesting. What was your name again?"

Vickie ignored her and hunched her shoulders. Like she thought she was maybe doing the wrong thing, talking to Claire.

"Please go on."

"Okay," Vickie said slowly. "Anyway, a lot of people started to surround them, so it was hard to see, but maybe five, ten minutes later, I turned around and I saw Valerie walking to the front door of the nightclub. She was holding hands with that same guy. You know, the one who teased her and scared her? Then they were gone."

Claire could hardly breathe.

Take it easy.

"Ms..."

"Monroe," the young girl said.

"Ms. Monroe, one of my close friends is a detective with the Dallas Police Department, and I would love for you to talk to him."

"Oh, no. I can't. I thought if I just told you..." She paused. "You can tell him for me." Vickie turned, as if she would flee.

"Wait," Claire said, trying not to give away how important this was. "See, they really need a description of the guy."

"Look, I'm telling you this just to help out. She acted like she knew the guy. Okay?" She leaned into Claire. "Look, I'm only nineteen. If my parents find out about this, I'm dead. I mean it. They're Evangelical, and they would rather me be dead than step foot in a nightclub."

Claire reminded herself to tread lightly. "Look, we need you so bad. Valerie was a friend and co-worker. You might be able to stop this vicious killer, who has already killed one of my friends and may have another friend and co-worker with him now."

"I can't. I'm having dinner with my grandparents, and I can't be late. I will call you tomorrow."

Obviously this girl was living in a different world. "Hey, here's my cell number. What's your number?"

The girl rattled it off, but Claire knew it was fake. The girl jogged off, then ran to the back parking lot behind the police station.

"Wait!" Claire called, trying not to make a scene in front of the other media and different people hanging around. She gave chase, and saw Vicki Monroe slide down the underpass where another adjoining parking lot was.

Someone grabbed Claire's arm and yanked her to a stop.

"What are you doing? It's not safe for you to run off like that."

"Chandler, let go," Claire screamed. "We have to find that girl. She said she saw the guy who left with Valerie." She yanked free and took off.

"What are you talking about?" Chandler was on her heels.

As Claire slid down the cement embankment, she stopped at the bottom just in time to see a white Volkswagen tear out of the parking lot. Claire shook her head. "Oh, this is just great. What kind of reporter are you?"

Chandler jogged up behind her. "Claire, you need to get a grip."

"Shut up, Chandler. First Jessica, then Melissa, now Valerie has disappeared. I've put up with your crap long enough. Leave me alone. I need to call Lance." Claire pulled out her cell phone. She needed to call Lance, but she was not going to do it in front of Chandler. She started walking back to the embankment, looking up wondering if there was another way back into the police station. She needed to get to Lance now.

Valerie's picture continued to be flashed across all of the television stations in Dallas and the surrounding areas. An urgent call for anyone who last saw her, referred people to call the Dallas police.

During the meeting with the FBI, a call came in from a bartender at the Knox Avenue Bar and Grill. He said he saw Valerie leave with a man, and, he could describe what he looked like. Lance had already talked to some of the news people who were there last night, but no one remembered anyone strange or different.

He'd checked the list of names. Still need to talk to a couple more people.

As Lance headed out with Reid, the FBI, and other detectives, Detective Davis Scott took a call from the Assistant Warden unit at Huntsville. He said the prisoner Watson claimed his twin brother drugged and switched identities with him and that he was out free.

The guy was throwing a fit. Davis tried to reach Lance on his cell phone. This was the craziest thing he'd ever heard of. Davis left a message for Lance on his cell and on his direct line to call him immediately.

"Fan out and question everyone," Lance ordered as their small group descended on the club. It was close to seven when Lance's cell phone rang. He excused himself, leaving Reid to finish the questioning.

"Claire, are you okay?"

"I'm good. Lance, a young woman was waiting for me after the six o'clock newscast here at the police station. I walked over and introduced myself." Claire paused, taking an audible breath in his ear. "She said she saw the guy Valerie left with from the nightclub."

"What are you saying?"

"She saw him, without the hoodie and face covering."

"Don't let her leave. I will be right there."

"Wait, that's the thing, she took off and I chased after her."

"Do you have her name and number? Quickly please."

"Yes, Vickie Monroe. She was short, long blonde hair, nineteen years old. She took off in a white Volkswagen."

"Shit, Claire, stay right there at the station. I'm on my way back."

Lance jogged back to the circle of people. They hadn't really gotten anywhere with the bartender; he served a hundred people or more a night. Hopefully, this might help his recall. He leaned in to Reid.

"Let's go. Claire talked to a girl who saw the guy Valerie left with. Tell Ryan and the rest of the gang to continue on," Lance didn't wait. He went for the front door of the club.

CHAPTER THIRTY

It was Thursday night, around 7:30 pm, when Lance, Reid and Davis entered the police station to see Claire sitting at the front talking to the desk officer. She looked exhausted.

"Claire, follow me."

They went down the hallway, into a room that looked gothic—with photographs of victims on a board and a whiteboard with a caravan of information on it from beginning to end.

Claire had already given the producer the updated information to lead in to her story for the ten newscast. She'd also talked to the News Director earlier about having Julie fill in for her.

Earlier, Chandler had left the police station, seething when Claire refused to let him stay with her. "You might need a photographer if something breaks—remember, live television news, that's what you do."

"No, Chandler, John said for you to come back, and to get with Julie. I'll call her with any additional information that I have before the ten newscast if there's more than what I already told Hillary. I'll be in early to do an update. I will see you tomorrow." Claire shooed him to the live truck. She didn't care that he was mad at her.

At the police station, Claire was seated in front of a room

full of detectives. Claire told them what had happened between her and the young lady. She was embarrassed she let the young woman slip away.

"We'll be in touch," Lance said.

Claire let Lance walk her to her car.

"I don't want you alone tonight. I can't come over. I have to stay here. I want to place an officer at your house."

"No way in hell, Lance. I'm a big girl. I'm actually going to get my gun out of my locked cabinet and sleep with it, just so you know. If anyone tries to come in my house, I will shoot them. Call me before you come over, if you are able to come over."

"It's a good thing you told me, in case I can get out early and can come over. If not, call me when you go to bed," Lance smiled. Claire thought how she loved his smile, he had her heart, as Lance hugged her.

Claire's mind was spinning out of control, even before she pulled away. She was more upset about Valerie than she cared to admit, and she prayed the police were able to find the young woman in the white Volkswagen.

She would have to wait to hear from Lance on what information she could use for the morning newscast. Hillary knew to expect her no matter what –she'd be doing an update on Valerie for sure.

Claire also wanted to find out what was going on with Chandler. Maybe he was having girlfriend trouble.

Lance was back in her life.

In between her worries, Lance was in her thoughts, last night and the night before, and all that'd happened between them. It had felt perfect, and she hoped that they could make it through this horrible ordeal. No, she knew they could, she and Lance were meant to be.

Maybe they would get a chance to be a real couple. She wanted forever, but Claire wasn't stupid. There was too much drama going on in their lives to know what was real or not.

Claire pulled into her garage. She remembered her cell was in her pocket.

She tried to call Lance. He didn't answer, so she hung up. Claire gathered up her belongings. She'd already taken her shoes off. Her stomach growled. She needed something, wine, a sandwich, something that might calm her nerves so she could think about tomorrow morning. She'd even check the mail later. What she wanted now was to get her gun out of the cabinet, get something to eat, and sink into a bubble bath.

Claire checked her locks. She couldn't help it. She froze when she heard a noise. It was coming from her bedroom.

Fear gripped her immediately, her heart dipped to her stomach.

Someone was in her house.

She pulled out her cell phone, dialed 911 and whispered to the dispatcher.

The dispatcher replied, "Please leave the house now."

Watson didn't hear Claire in the house until she was checking the locks on the doors for the second time. He froze. This was going to happen faster than he'd wanted. He couldn't jump off of her balcony. He'd break something if he did. It was now or never.

He'd convince her of his innocence. He'd tell her all the information the police didn't release about the first Smiley Face murders, and why it was happening again. Watson would take Claire to his secret place.

Watson had his idiot brother buy a lake house before he had come to see him at Huntsville. He had the keys and they were going to go there.

Claire walked slowly up the stairs. She was almost to her bedroom door. She could hear the dispatcher telling her to get away, again. For some reason she was drawn to see the person who had violated her privacy. She was so mad she could barely think. Understanding now how people who were so angry or felt violated and scared could kill, hit her in a wave.

CHAPTER THIRTY-ONE

Lance and Reid met with the computer specialists and sketch artists about the young woman witness they were searching for. They walked into controlled chaos in the conference room, computer keyboards clicking, beeping sounds, two television screens blaring the latest news and a group of cops and analysts in deep discussion about the investigation.

Detectives were on computers, production screens had been set up and turned on, photos of the male employees at KABC, provided by the general manager, were flashing through the criminal database to see if there were any matches to any past crimes.

Another section of detectives was working solely on trying to find a white Volkswagen registered in Dallas that would fit the description provided by Claire.

"Horne, how's it going?" Lance asked the FBI agent.

"I'm nearly finished. We are still looking for the Volkswagen, and I should have something for you in a couple of hours."

"I just hope we find Valerie alive," Lance said. "You're doing a great job. We're going back to the nightclub, and I'll check with you when we're done."

Out in the back of the police department, Lance and Reid took his truck and headed over to the nightclub.

Detective Ryan had just gotten into his Ford sedan with his partner Davis when the call came in. He knew it was Claire's house.

They were only ten blocks away. He turned his siren on and told the dispatcher they were on their way.

Davis called Harris again and told the dispatcher to alert all of the officers of a possible hostage situation, involving television news reporter Claire McKenzie. On his way to Claire's house, he continued to call Lance.

Mad at Claire, Chandler was at the nightclub where Valerie was abducted two days ago, sitting at the bar nursing a beer, and watching the Dallas detectives interview everyone.

He'd checked in at the station, they didn't need him for the ten newscast, and he'd learned from the producer, Hillary, that Claire was at the police station. They wouldn't tell him why. That was what led him to the beer break.

The detectives must've figured someone had already talked to him, because they were leaving him alone. He felt eyes on him and whirled on the barstool.

Detective Harris was staring. Chandler wasn't scared. He could kill Harris for what he was doing to Claire again, using her just like before.

Claire had mentioned they'd had dinner together last night. When he'd seen her at work this morning, it was obvious it was more than that, because he was watching, disgusted by the way she was acting, flitting around the newsroom.

Harris would pay for this.

Now, the detective had the balls to come across the bar towards him.

The guy stopped in his tracks when his cell phone went off, and Harris turned to take the call.

Within moments, the detective left with the other detectives.

What the hell?

Chandler followed, flipping on his police scanner in the news truck. Thinking like a news photographer now. It was time for new video and a new news story.

Claire made it to the top of the stairs. For a moment she felt foolish, thinking her woman's intuition had gotten the better of her, having just called 911.

Now the troops would come and she'd look like an idiot. She pushed her bedroom door open and a big arm grabbed her around the neck, dragging her inside her room. The door slammed shut. She was shoved onto her bed.

She was stunned when she realized who it was. He had a gun. Johnny Watson was supposed to be in prison!

Then everything went black.

Carrying her out down the stairs proved hard for Watson, because he'd gained some weight while he was in Huntsville. He'd bribed several officers to keep them from forcing him to go to exercise time in the workout room.

He got Claire in the back seat of his three-year-old Cadillac that had been secretly stashed during the trial. He'd parked it on the street behind her house.

He quickly drove away. It would take about forty minutes to get to his new secret lake house at Lake Texoma, and that would only give those bumbling idiot police enough time to get things moving at Claire's house.

As he turned on the access road toward the ramp to Interstate 45, he could hear the sirens in the background.

"Oh, my! Just missed it!" He flipped to a country station on the radio. He glanced back at Claire in the back seat, but she was still out cold. He had tied up her feet and hands. Watson chuckled to himself and put his blinker on to take the ramp east 75.

Once they arrived, Watson dragged Claire into his lake house. The lights were already on as if expecting him—thanks to his ex-lawyer. His neighbors hopefully didn't think anything unusual, just that someone had been living here for a while.

He was calm as he tied Claire to a makeshift large chair that resembled a huge picnic table with the back covered. Claire slowly woke up and then shuddered as she realized she was tied down. Her anger boiled over.

"I have to talk to you. You must listen to me. I'm innocent. The police didn't reveal all of the information about the murders. It's the Smiley Face Killer again. Harris already came to see me, blaming me for the murders, saying I had someone, an accomplice, working with me, and he threatened me to tell him who, but I was in prison and it's not me. I swear I'm innocent."

"How did you get out?" Claire screamed.

"My twin brother. I switched with him."

Claire jumped up and tried to charge into Watson, but to no avail. She was bound to the chair he had her in. Instead, she ended up toppling, along with the huge chair. It crashed down on her side, sending her into unconsciousness again.

Lance got the call about Claire from Detective Glen. He rushed out of the nightclub, vowing to talk to Jeremy Chandler as soon as he could. Claire was more important.

Claire's News Director, Carlson, had been trying to find her. He'd become concerned and started harassing the police with unending phone calls.

Police, SWAT, Lance and Reid, broke into Claire's house. She wasn't there.

Her neighbor, Ralph, walked over from next door and told the patrol officer he needed to talk to the person in charge. Ralph told Lance about the young man who'd recently rented the neighbor's house and how they all thought it was strange for a young person in an older neighborhood. They moved down the street to the old house and broke in, as part of

Claire's investigation. The police found all kinds of surveillance equipment, cameras, and computers. They found paperwork that proved Watson was there.

CSI detectives were everywhere and police computer specialists were called in.

There must have been hours of surveillance video of Claire's house, but Lance didn't have time to go through it—he had to find Claire. One computer guy came across an e-mail from Watson's attorney from a week ago just as Davis ran into the huge family room, telling Lance about the NYPD detective that was looking for him.

"I want Watson's attorney contacted now, dammit. Tell him if he doesn't tell us everything, he's going to be hauled in and charged with assisting a prison escape," Lance yelled at two detectives.

After talking to Watson's lawyer, he told the detectives about the house at Lake Texoma.

"Give me the address," Lance demanded as he headed towards the front door with Sanchez, Davis, and Ryan right behind him. "I want the son-of-a-bitch picked up now."

Lance recognized the New York area code on his phone and answered it as he hopped in his truck. As he started the engine, Sanchez jumped in, and they took off.

"Chief Harris, Andrew Simpson with NYPD. I know this sounds crazy, but after hearing this lady's account, she may have a wild story, but she has brought in documentation connecting Watson and her boyfriend, and she says it is his brother. She claims that Watson, on death row in Texas, switched with her boyfriend, the brother, and now he is in prison in Huntsville, Texas and Watson is out."

Lance froze. "Shit. Listen, Simpson, thanks. I'll need to get back with you. We have a hostage situation underway."

"What was that?" Sanchez asked.

"That son-of-a-bitch Watson does have her. I'm sure of it,

and they are at the lake house," Harris yelled. "Oh, shit, dispatch. I've got to take it. Call Oklahoma Police and tell them to meet us there. We have a hostage situation."

"Harris, I'm going to patch you through to the Huntsville Corrections Warden. He has information about Watson," the dispatcher said.

"Sir, Harris here."

"Detective Harris, Warden Juan Benavidez. I have determined that Johnny Watson has indeed escaped, and I'm getting ready to send out a nationwide bulletin to police and the news media. I wanted you to know first."

"I'll have to get the details from you later. I think we know where he is. I'll let you know." Harris hung up without a reply and handed his cell phone to Reid, who remained quiet as Lance hit the speedometer close to ninety mph.

"Reid, try Claire again."

His buddy didn't have to say anything. Lance knew the call went to voicemail.

Chandler drove up in his Corvette, and saw lights on. He could faintly hear sirens and quickened his step. He didn't have a lot of time. He grabbed his Glock from his console between his seats and jumped out.

He ran up to the huge front window. The curtains were sheer, and he could see Claire tied to a chair and Watson yelling at her.

Chandler crouched by the front door, counted to three and kicked the door in.

"Police!" he yelled.

Watson turned.

Claire screamed.

Watson shouted at Chandler and darted toward him.

"Watson, stop or I will shoot," Chandler said.

"It was you—it was you all along," were the last words out of Watson's mouth. Chandler took aim, pulled the trigger, and

Watson crumpled to the floor. A smoking hole between his eyes. A pool of blood started forming beneath him.

Claire was still screaming and crying.

Chandler could hear the sirens pulling up, and he ran to Claire, untying her just as Harris and the SWAT team rushed the house.

"Police! Drop your weapon. Don't move, asshole!" Harris yelled. "Take him."

Several officers grabbed Chandler and pulled him away from Claire.

She'd fallen to the floor. "No, Lance! Chandler saved me."

Lance picked her up, and pinned her to his chest.

She was sobbing so hard she could barely talk.

"Claire, are you okay? What the hell is going on here?"

Several officers descended on the house, making sure there was no one else in the house. Shortly, the paramedics arrived. They came inside and Reid motioned toward Watson, lying in a heap on the floor.

Chandler was handcuffed and pushed up against the wall.

Claire was trying to talk between her sobs.

"Claire, are you okay?"

"Yes," she whispered. "Bruised."

"Let's have the paramedics look at you, then you can tell me what happened." Lance motioned for two of the emergency squad to take Claire. "Lance, Chandler saved me. He came in and shot Watson," Claire said.

"Okay." Lance patted her back. "I will be right with you."

The paramedics took Claire off to the ambulance. Lance turned and took a swing at Chandler. In his gut he knew Chandler was danger and that was why he had his detectives and friend at the FBI investigating his background. Something wasn't right and he knew it. Chandler ducked, and Reid grabbed Lance's arms. His partner held him back. It was a good thing.

"What the hell are you doing here? Why didn't you call the police, you son of a bitch?" Lance hollered.

"Hey, jerk. I'm the one who saved her."

Lance broke free from Reid's hold, and launched his fist into Chandler's stomach. He fell to his knees, groaning.

Three other officers grabbed Lance to hold him off.

"Harris, stop. He's not worth it," Reid said.

"I want to know what this asshole is doing here."

"Hold him back," Reid said to the officers as he walked over to Jeremy Chandler, who was still on the floor.

"I'm damn sure pressing charges against that bastard," the guy spat.

"Don't know what you are talking about," Reid said as additional officers pulled Chandler to his feet.

Reid got in his face. "You heard the detective. We want to know why you're here. You are going to damn well tell us how you knew Watson had Claire here."

Lance watched, letting Reid handle things so he could calm down.

"Look, I have a police scanner. I'm the media, remember? I heard the address and knew it was Claire. Then, as I was on my way I heard about the discovery of Watson renting the house a couple of doors down from Claire. I knew he had her, and I knew about the house at the lake, and I knew that is where he would take her, so I headed this way."

"You broke the law. You should've called 911 immediately. Have him checked by the paramedics, then I want him taken in."

The officers dragged Chandler toward the front door when the KABC News Director Carlson, Claire and Chandler's boss, their attorney and the news media entourage tried to walk in.

By now, the officers had let go of Lance. He was still so angry he could barely breathe, even though he'd taken it down a notch. "I want that asshole charged with everything we got on him." Lance said.

"That won't be possible, Detective Harris."

"And who the hell are you?"

"I'm the KABC attorney, Marshall Folk. I am representing Jeremy Chandler and Claire McKenzie, and due to their injuries they will not be questioned tonight, but will gladly come into the police station in the morning."

The room is quiet.

"We can come to the hospital, and you can't stop us," Reid said.

Reid nodded towards Lance.

"I want Chandler there at eight in the morning. If he's one minute late I will have him arrested. Do you understand me, Mr. Folk?"

"Yes, detective. I'll have him there in the morning. If you will excuse me."

By now, the police crime scene specialists were getting the crime scene set up and gathering evidence.

"I have to check on Claire. I'll be right back." Lance headed out, only to see Chandler holding Claire's hands. He growled under his breath.

Claire ran into Lance's arms.

Lance held Claire tight. She felt so small against him and he didn't ever want to let her go. He didn't care that people were staring at him and Claire.

"Claire, I don't know what to say. I'm relieved you're alive, and once this is over it's going to be you and me. We'll take off on vacation and get back to where we were before," Lance whispered.

Claire was softly crying. "I want you, you and me. Forever."

"Forever, Claire," holding her close, knowing he would never let go. Unfortunately, back to reality. "What did the paramedics say?" He rubbed his hands softly up and down her back, still holding her close.

"I want to go home and get some rest," she said, keeping her voice low. "I have bruising, but they don't think I need to go to the hospital. I can't take it."

"I'll have one of the officers take you to my sister's. I will call her right now. The police have a crime scene at your house set up, so this will be the best. I will be there as soon as I can. Do you know where your cell phone is?"

"No." Claire stepped back to look into Lance's face.

Lance saw her boss, the News Director approaching. With his arm still around her, he put his hand out to Carlson.

"I'm glad Claire and Chandler are not hurt. This could have been a horrible scene," Carlson said after their shake.

"Yes, sir. And I need to get back to it. Do you have a cell phone you can give Claire? I'm going to have one of the officers take her to my sister's."

"Here, Claire, you can take my cell. I have another one," Claire's boss said.

Lance kissed Claire's forehead. "Call me so I'll have the number. I'll see you soon."

"I'll see you in a little while at your sister's," Claire leaned up and pressed her mouth to his.

Lance hid his surprise and kissed her back, but kept it much shorter than he would've liked. God, he loved this woman. He pulled back gently. "I'll send an officer right over, Claire."

He didn't have to say anything more.

She could tell by the look on his face, Lance blamed himself for what happened. Claire watched as he walked off.

Claire hoped Lance knew he was her hero, and if he didn't, she'd make sure he did later tonight.

"Claire, I am glad you are safe," Carlson said, which jolted her out of her head. "I'm devastated by everything that's happened to you and our news family. Why don't I tell the officer I'll take you to Lance's sister's house, so we can talk?"

Claire hesitated, since Lance wouldn't know she'd left with her boss instead of an officer.

She didn't have a chance to make a decision.

"I'm Tim Carlson, News Director at KABC and Claire's boss. I don't mind taking her where she needs to go."

"Detective Harris told me to take Ms. McKenzie to her destination."

"It's okay." Claire just wanted to leave. "I'll call Detective Harris and tell him."

"Thank you, ma'am."

Before she could call Lance, several co-workers ran up to her, forming a circle, all talking at once.

Carlson announced they'll have to talk to Claire tomorrow, so he could take her home.

Chandler was there, too, and put his arm around her as the talking continued.

"Thank you for saving my life," Claire said.

"You're welcome. Glad to be there for my favorite news reporter."

Claire smiled.

"Carlson, is it okay with you if I take Claire where she needs to go?" Chandler asked.

"I guess that'll work. I can get back to the television station and figure out what the hell we're going to do for the morning news. Did the paramedics clear you to go?"

"Yes."

"Goodbye, Claire, get some rest."

Claire was so tired, she didn't argue. She dialed Lance's number on her boss' cell phone. Before she could speak, Chandler leaned over and moved her toward his car.

"Let's get out of here," he said as he hung up the phone. Claire didn't even notice that Chandler had taken the phone out of her hands. She just slid into his Viper and in moments was sound asleep.

Chandler slid in and started the engine, changed to reverse and pulled away from the lake house. It would take him around an hour, he figured, to get to his house.

CHAPTER THIRTY-TWO

Chandler glanced, ever so often at Claire, as he drove back to downtown Dallas. He pulled into his condominium parking lot.

"Claire," he said softly, as he woke her up. "I needed to stop by my place before I take you. Is that okay?"

Everything was foggy. She didn't remember giving Lance's sister's address to Chandler. She let him pull her up out of the car.

"Okay, I guess. Then I really need to get going. Did I give you the address?"

"Yes. I will make us a quick sandwich, and then we can be on our way."

A glance at her watch told Claire it was after two in the morning. She wasn't hungry but didn't have the energy to do anything but nod. Chandler was a guy, and probably always hungry.

It'd been a long time since she'd been in his downtown loft, and she'd forgotten how sophisticated it was for a guy. Actually, *fancy* when she thought about it.

Chandler held her as they walked inside his place. It smelled good, like a home cooked meal.

Claire had forgotten that he enjoyed cooking, too. She'd eaten here a couple of times, but things had been so busy at work they hadn't had any down time together in a long time.

And, of course, there was Lance back in her life, so it would never go any further between her and Chandler.

Claire had told him that before.

As they entered the large living room, Claire glanced over to one side of the room that held all of Chandler's electronic devices, including two computers and several cameras, all different kinds, and an editing system.

She noticed on one of the shelves there was an eight by ten picture of her and Chandler. Melissa had taken it the night after their first exclusive story.

Claire and Chandler had huge smiles on their faces. It made her sad to look at it.

"Make yourself at home while I make us some sandwiches."

She sat down on one of the couches, but looked over at the computer so she could check her e-mail and the local news websites for the latest news information.

"Chandler, I am going to borrow one of your computers," Claire called.

Chandler didn't answer, even after a few minutes, so she figured he'd heard her and didn't care. He wouldn't mind anyway.

She sat down at the first office chair and rolled over to the computer. Claire remembered Chandler laughing and telling her a long time ago, *"My mind is always on getting the photograph perfect, so I don't ever use fancy passwords for my computer. Nope, it's always my last name and my age."*

As the computer screen came to life, Claire typed, Chandler27. As the computer cleared the password and the first images popped up, she froze.

Her chest tightened and she couldn't breathe.

CHAPTER THIRTY-THREE

It was around two in the morning when Lance and his crew began winding down. The evidence and crime scene officers were still at it.

He told the sergeant in charge they were taking off, and to call him if he needed anything. As Lance headed toward Reid to tell him they could leave, he pulled out his cell and glanced at the screen. He frowned. There was a missed call, but, he hadn't heard it ring.

He noticed the phone number wasn't in his contacts, but figured it was Claire calling from her boss' cell phone to leave him the number. He checked the voicemail just in case, and stopped in his tracks as he heard a man's voice say, "Let's get out of here."

Lance recognized the voice. He saved the voicemail and called his sister's house. Julie sounded like she'd been sound asleep, even though she'd answered on the third ring.

"Let me speak to Claire," Lance demanded.

"She's not here yet," his sister said. "I fell asleep on the couch waiting for her."

"Shit."

"I'm sending an officer there now. Don't answer the door unless you know for sure it's the cops."

"What's wrong?" Reid asked, as his partner closed the

distance between them.

Lance held his hand up. He was already dialing dispatch. "I need a patrol officer sent to my sister's house immediately. Claire never showed up." He rattled off the address and hung up. Lance still didn't pause to answer Reid. He dialed the newsroom, a number he'd had saved in his cell phone, Carlson's direct line. His cell phone was next if he didn't answer.

"KABC Newsroom. May I help you?"

"This is Detective Harris calling for News Director Tim Carlson."

"I am sorry, he is in a meeting."

"You get him on the phone right this minute. This is a police matter."

The girl, who'd sounded young, put him on hold. He didn't have to wait long for Carlson.

"Detective, what's up?"

"Did the officer take Claire somewhere?"

"No, we told him I was going to take her to your sister's. Then at the last moment Chandler offered. It worked out so I could come back to the newsroom and wait to hear from you guys so we could decide what to do for the morning newscast."

"Claire never showed up at my sister's, and that was two hours ago. I want Chandler's address right now."

"Let me get it for you," Carlson said as Harris listened to him call out to the news staff there for Chandler's address. "Just a moment," as he put Harris on hold.

"What's going on, Harris?" Reid barked. Obviously his partner didn't like being ignored, if the dark look on his lined face was any indication.

Lance looked Reid straight in the eyes, the anger and determination clear.

"Not only do we know who the Smiley Face Killer is, the bastard, Jeremy Chandler, has Claire."

Lance was running at this point, even though one of the crime scene officers was yelling for him. Reid's expression changed to hate and he raced after Harris.

Carlson came back on the phone. "2823 Beaumont Avenue. It's a condo loft in downtown Dallas, number 65."

Lance ended the call without another word. The last thing he needed was for Claire's boss to start questioning him.

He and Reid jumped in his truck, and he gave the dispatcher Chandler's address.

"I'm ordering the SWAT team and anyone else available to this address right now. Television news photographer Jeremy Chandler lives there, and he should be considered armed and dangerous."

"You always had a bad feeling about Chandler," Reid said as Lance hit ninety-five miles per hour entering the freeway to downtown Dallas.

"And I need my ass kicked for not following up sooner. Now Claire may be in trouble because of it. If he hurts her, I'll kill him."

CHAPTER THIRTY-FOUR

Claire stared at the images on the screen. Most of the photographs were of her, but there were also pictures of Melissa and other girls. They appeared to be in a filthy basement or a room.

She saw Valerie and felt her fear as she looked in her eyes. All of these girls had been abused and were dying or were already dead. Then she saw the photograph that stunned her. Jenny Latham, staring back at her. Movement had her head whipping over her shoulder.

He's coming!

Claire had to run for her life.

Chandler was humming to himself as he put the sandwiches on a tray and two glasses of wine. From here on out, it would be him and Claire. He'd saved her life, and she would go with him anywhere to work at another television station, far away from Dallas.

"Why not CNN?" He chuckled.

They were a great team.

He stopped in his tracks when he saw Claire staring at the computer, studying images that were for his own private use.

"What the hell are you doing, Claire?"

She jumped and ran to the door.

Chandler dropped the tray and beat her there, putting her

in a choke hold.

"You dumb bitch! We could've have had it all! You've ruined everything! It was supposed to be different with you, Claire!" Chandler yelled. "We're getting out of here now."

He dragged Claire to his desk and grabbed his keys. Then he heard a commotion from outside his front door. He could hear the elevator doors opening, and the *ding* that announced it.

"Time to say goodbye, Claire." Chandler punched her in the face, and she slumped in his arms, her pretty head falling to one side. Well, at least his emergency exit off of the balcony would finally come in handy. Chandler lifted Claire, putting her over his shoulders, and headed out the glass doors.

He was already in the parking lot, laying Claire down in the back seat when he heard additional sirens.

Chandler jumped in his Viper, started the engine and without his lights on and the engine idling, he slowly crept out another secret exit he knew about that would give him the time he needed to get to Lake Dallas and to his getaway car.

Lance was yelling at Davis on his cell phone as he drove like a bat out of hell down the Interstate. Two state troopers were behind him, signaling for other officers not to stop him.

"You wake up those computer geeks who are supposed to be such geniuses and get them on Jeremy Chandler, the news photographer at KABC who has kidnapped Claire McKenzie, the news reporter. I want everything on him and any additional properties he may be paying taxes on, besides this condo. We are in Dallas. Get it on, Davis, now. Call the FBI and wake their asses up. We need them."

Reid took his cell phone and called dispatch next. "Put me through to the SWAT lead."

"Campbell."

"Sanchez here, we are five minutes out, did you get Claire McKenzie?"

"No, sir, we found a secret exit off of the balcony. We have checked the parking lot, everywhere. They're gone."

"Be there in five."

Lance slowed onto the downtown exit. He jerked his truck to a stop in front of the condos. His cell screamed and he dived for it from Reid's hand.

It was his FBI buddy.

"Harris, found something, Chandler has a house at Lake Dallas, fifteen minutes away, 102 Hart Street. We're on our way."

"That's only about ten minutes away. How did you find it?"

"Oh, one of the computer geeks we dragged out of bed found it on Chandler's computer at his loft."

Harris hung up. With his truck lights blinking emergency, he tried to keep his truck below sixty on the streets of downtown Dallas as he headed to the lake.

Reid, hadn't said a word, was probably preparing for what they were going to run into and setting up the rescue in his mind.

Claire jolted awake, the smell was horrible, it smelled like feces and vomit and it filled her lungs. She could barely breathe. She was in a bedroom somewhere, and there were skeletons tied up and lying on the floor around the room. Claire noticed her clothes were ripped and falling off.

Then she spotted Valerie. Her friend was leaning her head against the bed. Valerie was tied up. She looked dead, but Claire noticed her nose and mouth move.

"Valerie, oh my god, what is this?"

Valerie opened her eyes but could not move her mouth. She must've been so dehydrated she didn't have the strength to tell her anything. Her hands were tied. Tears ran down Claire's face.

Claire prayed for Valerie, her family, friends but mostly for

Lance. She hoped he could survive this. She daydreamed about what it would be like to marry Lance. Her parents would love him. What would it be like to have his children, our children?

Claire choked, and tears fell down her face. She'd never have Lance's child, her own baby boy or girl. To watch her son play football or baseball or her daughter be a cheerleader or softball player.

The door slammed open, and Chandler was standing there, a small suitcase in one hand.

"Come on, Claire, we are out of here." He dropped the suitcase and stalked to Claire, sitting on the floor beside a desk in the bedroom.

"Why?" Claire sputtered.

"I claimed you the first day you walked in to the newsroom, but you disobeyed me when you went with Harris. That doesn't happen to the Chandler men. We get the women we want. No one is ever going to find you. I have a car parked down by the lake with the license plates registered to a dead family member. No one will ever find us in Alaska."

Chandler hit her again, and everything went black.

Lance, Reid, Davis and Ryan reached the house in Lake Dallas. The whole place was dark. They quietly moved to the front door, guns pulled, getting ready for the operation of kicking in the door and saving Claire.

He was impatient, but he had to hold on and remember his training if he was going to save her.

What the other detectives didn't know, was he was going to kill Chandler, no matter what. Even if he had to spend the rest of his life in prison.

They descended on the dark house, knowing that Jeremy Chandler was the Smiley Face Killer.

Chandler had Claire slung over his shoulder. He was making his way out of the back of his house as he heard the police crashing into the front.

He walked slowly, not wanting to draw attention to himself, and of course the female body he had over his shoulder, although neighbors would probably think at this hour they were on their way to the lake for some fun in the sack.

He had to get away before the sun began to rise, and he was pressing it.

Claire will agree to my terms if she wants to live. Chandler didn't want to kill Claire. He loved her.

He heard a branch crack, as if someone was behind him, and he pulled his gun out. Chandler looked right into the eyes of the meanest detective he'd ever known.

Harris was pointing a gun at him.

Chandler slowly raised his Glock to Claire's head.

"Your choice, buddy. Your beautiful Claire or me."

Lance held his gun steady at Chandler's head. "I knew something wasn't right with you."

"You will never have her. She's mine."

Lance yelled. "Police, drop your weapon!"

Chandler had the nerve to laugh.

"No." He raised his gun higher, taking aim at Lance. "I told you, she's mine. We're leaving."

"Last chance."

"I told you, *No!*" Chandler pulled the trigger, but the shot went wild, over Lance's shoulder.

He ducked as he pulled the trigger, returning fire at the serial killer. He watched as Chandler fell and Claire rolled off his shoulder down the ridge.

Lance swore and ran to her. He knelt down to pick Claire up off the ground, checking to see if she was breathing.

Thank god.

That was when he noticed her bruised face. The anger in Lance exploded. He was glad he had killed Chandler.

"Chandler's dead. I called an ambulance, and the cavalry's

already on the way," Lance told Claire.

Reid raced in. "Police!"

"It's over," Lance yelled, as Reid and the SWAT behind him came in and stopped.

"I have to get you to the hospital," Harris said as he picked Claire up and started to carry her. He wasn't waiting for an ambulance. He'd take her himself.

EPILOGUE

Claire was in the hospital for forty-eight hours before she woke up. Lance never left her side, sitting in the chair beside her bed, holding her hand for hours at a time.

Reid kept him up to date on the Smiley Face Killer investigation.

What detectives and the FBI discovered about Chandler and his family made even the toughest cop physically ill.

The skeletal remains inside the basement were Chandler's mother, sister and father. Chandler's wealthy aunt and uncle had taken him in, thinking his family had been killed in a car accident. That was how he'd gone off to college at the University of Alabama and had been financially set for life with an account from his parents set up by his uncle.

Police were still trying to identify the other three female bodies found at the lake house.

Valerie survived her horrific ordeal. Chandler had everyone fooled. She'd told police she'd wanted to date him for a long time, and when he began to pay attention to her, she'd thought he was the one.

Her parents, Anita and Maurice, had said at a news conference the day she went home from the hospital, that Valerie planned to return to her job as a Channel Two news reporter and that she was recovering quite well.

Dallas Police Chief Ben Lewis held a news conference, unloading information Harris and Sanchez wish he had kept quiet about, but Lewis wanted the world to know what he had done to catch this deadly killer.

Dallas homicide detectives were still trying to piece together a timeline that included a connection to any missing women in the last ten years. They did finally confirm through their investigation that the aunt and uncle were also dead, they believe killed by Chandler.

No one in the media had been able to find out where Chandler's aunt and uncle had been buried. The news ratings for KABC television were outrageous.

Claire's News Director, Carlson, and many of her family, friends and co-workers, were stationed outside her room in the hall. Hillary was the one who said she wasn't leaving till she saw Claire again. Her parents were giving Lance a few moments with her alone before they planned to enter the room to see their daughter. Claire's father was having to hold up her mother for fear she would collapse. She was so terrified of what she had learned had happened to Claire.

Lance didn't care about any of it as he looked down at Claire's beautiful face.

He was going to marry Claire. He'd already made the decision for both of them.

She must've have been reading his mind, because she slowly opened her eyes.

Claire was looking at the most handsome, strongest man in the world. Lance was her hero.

He leaned over and folded his arms around her.

"Claire, you look so beautiful," as he held her close to him. Lance was never going to let her go.

"Help me up and sit next to me," Claire said. "Why Chandler?" Claire whispered. "I never knew."

"Claire," Lance said, "you need to know that we are

continuing our investigation into Chandler and the murders. We found evidence that Chandler may not have been working alone."

Claire went silent as she tried to take in what Lance had just told her. Claire and Lance continued sitting on the bed, holding each other. Forever, Claire knew.

ACKNOWLEDGMENTS

You will enjoy the main characters in my mystery fiction novel **Beyond the Shadows,** Television news reporter, Claire McKenzie, Dallas Police Detectives, Lance Harris, Reid Sanchez, television engineer, Greg and television intern journalist, Melissa, as they set the stage for the journey. One of the main messages, always have faith and never give up.

In **Beyond the Shadows,** I hope for everyone to experience that there is always hope no matter what trials and tribulations are set in your path. The best of life is always there for you to grasp, always keep trying, stay focused and never give up following your dream.

Detectives Harris and Sanchez search endlessly for the serial killer terrorizing women on the streets of Dallas, Texas. Claire becomes entangled in the investigation when Lance discovers that Claire knows the killer personally, but she doesn't know this as she reports daily on the investigation and the latest news. Will Lance be able to save Claire before she becomes the killer's next victim?

What an incredible journey this has been getting **Beyond the Shadows** published! As a television journalist, I always knew I wanted to become a published author and I couldn't have made this incredible journey without the support of my husband, Greg, and my son, Spencer, who have always been there for me all along the way and helped me make my dream come true. Greg and Spencer, the two of you are my heroes!

Beyond the Shadows was the first novel I began writing and then I discovered I had cancer for the second time. I placed this novel aside as I went through my medical and chemotherapy treatments. During that time, I wrote and published my first novel, **'Family Secrets.'** I don't believe in coincidences. Through God's blessings, I survived chemotherapy treatments, regained my strength and was determined to make my day a fantastic journey. It was a blessing for me to return to writing **Beyond the Shadows,** especially because over the last ten years the technology and our lives have changed so much.

Thank you, family, friends and writers' group members, for all your support. You have always been a great source of encouragement. Thank you to my beautiful niece, Claire, for posing for the cover of my book. I want to thank my dearest, best friend, Tammy Landers, who helped edit **Beyond the Shadows** and has always been by my side.

As a television news journalist reporter, I covered and reported on two serial killer murder trials. The men were both convicted. I will never forget what happened after both trials. What you do as a reporter, you remove yourself from who you are, and you walk up and interview the convicted, horrible person and then when you walk away, you break down and return to who you are. The convicted killers both told me they were innocent. I knew that was not the truth. They were evil. I have videos of my stories and it still breaks my heart every time I look at them.

No matter what curves are thrown your way as you travel down the road of life, you must never forget that through your faith in God – you can survive.

All the best and enjoy reading!

DeAnn Daley Holcomb

www.deanndaleyholcomb.com

ABOUT THE AUTHOR

DeAnn Daley Holcomb is an award-winning television and print media journalist, published author, writer, editor, substitute teacher and public speaker. Her first novel, *Family Secrets*, was a finalist honored by the Eric Hoffer National Book Awards and Dan Poynter's EBook Awards. DeAnn's latest book is a mystery novel, *Beyond the Shadows*. DeAnn lives in Texas with her husband, Greg, and son, Spencer. If she's not working on her computer and writing, you can find her in Colorado enjoying the great beauty and outdoors. Check out her website at www.deanndaleyholcomb.com.

ABOUT ATMOSPHERE PRESS

Atmosphere Press is an independent, full-service publisher for excellent books in all genres and for all audiences. Learn more about what we do at atmospherepress.com.

We encourage you to check out some of Atmosphere's latest releases, which are available at Amazon.com and via order from your local bookstore:

Dancing with David, a novel by Siegfried Johnson

The Friendship Quilts, a novel by June Calender

My Significant Nobody, a novel by Stevie D. Parker

Nine Days, a novel by Judy Lannon

Shadows of Robyst, a novel by K. E. Maroudas

Home Within a Landscape, a novel by Alexey L. Kovalev

Motherhood, a novel by Siamak Vakili

Death, The Pharmacist, a novel by D. Ike Horst

Mystery of the Lost Years, a novel by Bobby J. Bixler

Bone Deep Bonds, a novel by B. G. Arnold

Terriers in the Jungle, a novel by Georja Umano

Into the Emerald Dream, a novel by Autumn Allen

His Name Was Ellis, a novel by Joseph Libonati

The Cup, a novel by D. P. Hardwick

The Empathy Academy, a novel by Dustin Grinnell

Tholocco's Wake, a novel by W. W. VanOverbeke

Dying to Live, a novel by Barbara Macpherson Reyelts

Surrogate Colony, a novel by Boshra Rasti

Orleans Parish, a novel by Chad Pentler

The Gift of Dragons, a novel by Rachel A. Greco